Avocado

Toast

The Orchard Brides Series
Book 1

Nancy Fraser
Best Selling & Award-Winning Author

Avocado Toast
The Orchard Brides, Book 1

COPYRIGHT © 2022 by Nancy Fraser
ISBN: 9798441092135

Cover by Black Widow Books © 2022

Avocado Toast

The Orchard Brides ~ Book 1

The last place Andrew (Drew) Morgan wants to be is back on the family avocado farm in Plentiful. If he had his way, he'd still be active military and deployed someplace far, far away. Unfortunately, he rarely gets what he wants. And, being back in the orchard is just the latest in a long list of disappointments.

Single mother, Chloe Taylor has relocated from Fresno to the rural area of Plentiful, California to build her marketing business beginning with the local agriculture co-op. It's her job to convince the local farms to invest in a major overhaul of the co-op's publicity campaign. A mixture of modern operations, and older, family-owned farms, only adds to her frustration.

At the moment, her biggest challenge is bringing the owner of Plenty Good Farms in line with the others. The fact that the old curmudgeon of an owner, Samuel Morgan, has brought his nephew in to run things gives her hope. Surely, the younger Morgan will be more amenable to her progressive ideas.

When Chloe first presents her plan the Morgan men, it's Drew who throws a monkey wrench into his uncle's agreement to sign the necessary contract. What she doesn't realize is that Drew's reluctance has more to do with his uncle's health issues, and the possibility that he won't be able to talk the man who raised him into retiring.

When Drew is forced by the military medical team into choosing between a desk job or retirement, he shares his frustrations with Chloe and she helps him find a new purpose outside of being a full-time farmer. It also helps that their attraction is growing. Drew has definitely fallen for the independent woman, and her adorable daughter.

Will Chloe's faith and determination help her lead Drew through his difficult decisions and bring them what they both need... a love that transcends their everyday challenges.

Praise for Author Nancy Fraser

Chapter One

Drew Morgan pulled his muddy four-wheeler to a stop on the side of the road just short of the driveway leading to Plenty Good Farms. The last place he wanted to be, but where he was needed most. After nearly twelve years of active military service, he understood duty. Responsibility.

It wasn't like the military was giving him an assignment any time soon. If ever.

He killed the engine, slid from behind the wheel, and walked around for a few minutes, working the kinks out of his bum leg and stretching his back. It wouldn't do to arrive on his uncle's porch with a limp.

The stubborn old coot would likely brand him injured and useless, and continue to insist he could manage on his own.

Drew knew better. Thanks to a letter from Doc Taylor, he'd been apprised of Sam's failing health. As badly as Drew wanted to stay close to Fort Hood in hopes of haranguing them into letting him go back to work, he couldn't very well desert the man who'd raised him from the age of ten.

C'mon, Andrew, grow a pair!

His uncle's familiar admonishment echoed in Drew's ears. Samuel Morgan was—if nothing else— an opinionated and cranky curmudgeon who liked nothing better than to goad people into doing what he wanted them to do.

Still, Drew loved the set-in-his-ways old man with all his heart. So much so, he'd accepted his mandatory three-month medical leave without so much as an argument. Then, he'd set out on the eighteen-hour drive from the base to the farming town of Plentiful, California in order to check on Sam for himself.

No sense putting off the inevitable any longer. Drew hopped back into the car and turned up the long, winding driveway. Parking at the rear of the century-old farmhouse, Drew took the steps two at a time, the reward for his exuberance a shooting pain that ran from behind his knee cap, up the back of his thigh, and ended in his hip. With the pain came the flash of memory he couldn't quite escape, the loud explosion of an IED, flames shooting into the air, jagged shards of shrapnel flying everywhere.

He stopped at the door and sucked in a breath before turning the knob and stepping into the warm and welcoming kitchen.

"About time you got here, Andrew," Sam groused from his seat at the table. He cradled an all-too-familiar cup of coffee in his sun-tanned grasp.

The first thing Drew noticed was the way Sam's hands trembled where he held the ceramic mug. "The road was wet," Drew countered. "I couldn't go top speed all the way."

Sam's faded gray gaze narrowed in his direction. "No doubt you've lost all the driving skills I taught you as a teenager."

"After maneuvering caravans of military vehicles for a dozen years, handling a lightweight four-wheel drive takes a bit of practice."

"Yeah, well, you're home now. You'll catch on once you're back on the tractor and pulling a wagon load of fresh-picked 'cados."

Drew poured himself a coffee from the old enamel pot on the stove and took a seat across from his uncle. "I suppose I will, for as long as I'm here."

"And just how long is that gonna be, boy?"

A shrug lifted his shoulders, and Drew explained, "Three months minimum, with regular checkups at the military-approved medical center in San Diego. Once they give me a final assessment, the higher-ups will let me know if I can go back to active duty or not."

"What are your other options?" Sam asked.

"I can go on desk duty. Or, I can put in my papers and retire."

"Riding a desk is for sissies. If those fools won't let you go back to serve where you're needed most, then I suppose I could make a spot for you here at the farm."

Drew bit the inside of his cheek to stifle his laugh. "I'd appreciate that, Sam. We've got some time to think about it."

"I could use your help with something even more pressing than the next harvest, though," Sam explained.

"What's that?"

Sam pushed a pile of papers across the table. "It's that danged woman down at the co-op. She's at it again. Buggin' us all to modernize our advertising. Use somethin' called Twipper and Instagripe."

"Twitter and Instagram," Drew corrected. Grinning, he added, "At least she hasn't asked you to create a TikTok. Yet."

"She's set up a new web-thingy with pictures of our farms and the surrounding countryside. Abel Marks says it looks nice, but I haven't seen it."

"I'll take out my laptop after supper. Maybe we can look at the website together. Just to see if the woman knows her stuff."

"Near as I can figure, 'bout all she knows is how to sweet-talk everyone into doing what she wants."

Sounds familiar, just without the 'sweet'.

"But not you, of course."

"Things are fine just the way they are," Sam argued. "Been this way for the past fifty-odd years since your great-grandpa started this farm. No sense rattling the trees that feed us." Sam took a long pull on his coffee, and added, "Besides, I ain't fallin' for no fancy sales pitch. The only sweet talkin' I'm interested in is coaxing them new Hass trees into bearing more fruit."

"How many varieties do you have now?" Drew asked. If there was one thing Sam loved, it was talking about his crops.

"Just three—Fuerte, Pinkerton, and Hass. I thought of adding a few of the Bacon strains to the south field, but we're doing perfectly fine with the usuals."

Drew inhaled deeply, finally noticing the wonderful aroma floating around the kitchen. His empty stomach growled in appreciation. "Something smells good. What's for supper?"

"Helen put on a roast before she left for the day. Got some carrots and potatoes in the pot too."

"She's still working for you? I'd have thought you'd have chased her off by now like all the others."

"Hmph. Don't think I haven't tried. She just shoots me that smirk of hers and goes on working."

Perhaps Sam had finally met his match. The thought gave Drew an internal chuckle. Given the household help that had come and gone over the past few years, Helen must truly be a gem. Or just as stubborn as Sam himself.

"So, what's on the schedule for tomorrow?" Drew asked.

"Church services in the morning. Then, maybe we should take a tour of the property and refresh your memory on what needs to be done. Since you're planning to stay a spell, that is."

"I wouldn't mind taking a drive through town," Drew added. "You can point out all the changes since I was here last."

"That'd be okay, I suppose. We can make a stop at the co-op building too. At least we won't run the risk of running into that crazy woman—it being Sunday and all."

"Crazy woman? You mean the marketing manager who's trying to drag you kicking and screaming into the twenty-first century?"

"Yeah, her. Even got a fancy name. Chloe. What kinda name is that anyway? I'll not be taking any advice from some upstart youngun with a weird name."

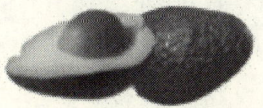

Chloe Taylor sorted through the last few co-op contracts, happy to see three of the five holdouts had finally signed on the dotted line. If they were going to make this work—rebrand and revitalize an area that was far off the recognition map—everyone had to come on board.

Even Sam Morgan.

The grumpy relic was her staunchest naysayer, a man badly in need of being dragged by his thumbs into the modern world of marketing.

She doubted Mr. Morgan even owned a computer, much less had internet out at that farm of his. If he could only see what she'd created. Appreciate the hard work she'd put into revitalizing the entire county, and especially the area known as Plentiful, then maybe he'd fall in line with the others.

Rumor around town was that his health was failing. Madelyn Pickard, bookkeeper for the co-op, had mentioned Sam's nephew was coming back to Plentiful to help him out with the spring harvest.

Perhaps the younger Morgan would be more amenable to her sales pitch. Maybe he'd hold more sway with his uncle than—what had Sam called her—a prissy city girl with high falutin ideas.

Who even talked like that anymore? Obviously, a man still stuck in the early to mid-twentieth century.

"Mom! Where's my backpack?"

Chloe turned away from her computer and met the frantic gaze of her eight-year-old daughter, Jessi. "Last time I saw it, the straps were draped over the arm of the chair in the family room."

"I just looked," Jessi assured her. "It's not there."

Chloe pushed herself to her feet intent on helping with the search. "I thought you'd finished your homework already."

"I did. But I left a granola bar and half a cheese sandwich in there, and I don't want it to get all gross."

Navigating an immediate U-turn, Chloe made her way to the corner of the spare bedroom. Jessi followed closely on her heels.

"There's your culprit."

"Boomer, no!" Jessi screeched. "Not my new backpack."

Strips of red corduroy material lay spread out on Boomer's dog bed. The only remaining sign of Jessi' cheese sandwich was the plastic baggy. The wrapper from the granola bar was torn to pieces with no more than a few crumbs left clinging to the shiny silver paper.

"That's the third one this school year," Chloe pointed out. "You've really got to be more careful what you leave in your bag, and where you hang it up when it's not in use."

"I'm sorry, mom. I'll use my birthday money to buy a new one."

"How about we split the cost?"

Eagerly, Jessi accepted. "That would be great. Thanks, mom."

"Go set out your clothes for church in the morning. Then, take your bath and get into your pajamas. We'll watch a movie before you go to bed."

"Can we have popcorn?"

"We'll see. Now scoot while I clean up this mess and pack away my laptop."

Once she's discarded the remnants of Boomer's thievery, Chloe returned to her desk in the cramped den and gathered up the signed contracts, adding them to the files for the Plentiful Fresh Food Cooperative. The two unsigned contracts were placed in her briefcase for her scheduled Monday meetings.

Her hard work on the co-op's website had finally turned Abel Marks around and she expected he'd sign at their nine o'clock appointment.

Then, with everyone else in place, she'd make yet another appeal to Sam Morgan. Surely a man who'd been in business for what seemed like forever wouldn't want to be left out in the cold to fend for himself when everyone else was benefiting from her aggressive campaign.

Would he?

Chapter Two

Drew pulled to a stop at the front entrance of the church and let Sam out before driving around to the parking lot. Standing there on the dark pavement, he turned and glanced out over the open fields of crops. Orchards of every kind. Apples, pears, oranges, lemons, pecans, and—right in the middle of everything—avocados.

Nothing much had changed in Plentiful since his last visit four years ago. Except, perhaps, for the chestnut-haired beauty standing next to the compact SUV on the opposite side of the long driveway. She'd not been here last time.

He would have definitely remembered her.

Drew made his way inside and took his seat beside Sam, second pew on the aisle, right hand side. The only time the position ever changed was if there was a funeral and the grieving family needed the first few rows. Even then, Sam sat as close to the front as possible.

'*As close to the Lord as I can get,*' Sam always

claimed.

Leaning in his uncle's direction, Drew whispered, "Is Reverend Watson still leading services?"

"Yep," Sam responded. "Man's even older than me. The Good Lord obviously likes his preaching."

Drew shifted in his seat, glancing around the small church, taking in the eclectic membership. Families sat together. The older ladies still wore what his late aunt Harriett had called '*Sunday-go-to-Meeting hats*'. Her own hats had been some of the most ornate. The younger couples sat next to their aging parents and grandparents. No doubt some had children of their own, all of whom would be upstairs in Sunday School.

He recognized quite a few of the faces, but definitely not all. Searching the crowd for the attractive brunette from the parking lot, he was disappointed when he couldn't find her among the parishioners. Perhaps she'd only been dropping someone off.

He was about to ask another question when the choir came out from the anteroom and took their seats. The reverend followed moments later and took his place at the pulpit.

Closing his eyes, Drew let the serenity of the familiar Sunday routine sink into his soul. This quaint, wood and stone sanctuary was a far cry from the makeshift tents in foreign countries where he'd spent his last twelve years giving praise.

There were definitely going to be some perks to his forced medical leave. The much-needed welcome of the church, the chance to work out in the fresh air alongside the only family he could remember, and—if he was shrewd about it—the possibility of talking Sam into retiring. Maybe even selling the farm. Or, at least, leasing it out so he could finally relax and enjoy the rest of his years rather than work from dawn until dusk.

Chloe arranged the older children in a circle around the huge rocking chair. Her two teenage helpers, Sara and Rose, tended to the three toddlers at the arts and crafts table. "Did everyone read the assigned passage from last Sunday?" Chloe asked.

A few hands shot up. More than few remained down.

"Matthew," Chloe said softly, handing the boy a box of crayons. "Will you please pass these out to the children here on the story rug? One crayon each."

The six-year-old jumped to his feet and took the orange box from her hands, eagerly sharing them among his friends. "What color do you want, Miss Chloe?"

She gave a shake of her head. "Color doesn't matter for this lesson. I'll take whatever is left when you're done."

Once the children were all in possession of a single crayon, Matthew returned to his usual spot at the foot of the rocker. The boy next to him, Carl, gave him a solid nudge to the side.

Drawing a breath, Chloe began the day's lesson. "Crayons are a fun way to create beautiful pictures. But there's also a problem with crayons." To make her point, she held up her crayon before snapping it in half. "They break. Very easily." She nodded toward Carl and, with a broad grin, the boy broke his crayon in the same way.

Chloe continued. "And the older you get, the easier it is to break your crayons. The bigger and stronger you are, the more careful you have to be if you don't want to break them all."

"I'm very careful with all my art supplies," Becca Peters announced proudly.

"That's good, Becca, because if you're not careful, pretty soon you won't have any crayons left. Or, just a bunch of pieces. You can still color with them, but it's not as easy or as much fun."

Murmurs of agreement floated around the

circle, urging her on. "We're a lot like crayons. We can be broken, if someone mistreats us. Some of you may know children who mistreat others. They think they can get what they want from those around them who are smaller, weaker, or just different than they are. They push others around. They call them names. They hurt a lot of people. Has anyone ever mistreated you like that?"

A few of the smaller children nodded.

"Unfortunately, bullies are everywhere. No matter whether it's at school, or even here at church, they leave broken people behind. The sad thing is that these bullies could have several friends if they wanted. But instead of trying to be nice to others, they push and shove and break those around them."

She turned her attention to a few of the older children who sat at the back of the circle. "How many of you think that bullies have any real friends?"

Tommy Jacobs spoke up. "I wouldn't want to be friends with a bully."

"We should all remember just how fragile these crayons are because, like I said, people are like crayons. Just as we take care of our toys—our crayons—we should also take care of others by treating them with kindness. I also hope you'll be more aware of those around you. Not just the bullies, but the people whom the bullies are mistreating. Nothing heals a broken child like a friendly show of friendship and support."

Letting her words sink in, she waited until the children were all looking directly at her before she added, "Don't forget, God wants us to love the bullies too. They may not look like it, but most of them are broken crayons as well. Show love and compassion to a bully and you could make a real difference in their life, and in yours."

Once the lesson was over, Chloe stood and waved the children to their feet for the closing prayer. She was about to ask for a volunteer, when Carl turned to Matthew and put his arm around the smaller boy's shoulders.

"I'm sorry I shoved you before. I didn't mean anything by it other than I was a bit cramped between you and Becca."

"It's okay," Matthew said in return. "I'm not a crayon. I didn't break."

Ten minutes later they were filtering out of the staircase leading from the classroom to the grassy field behind the church parking lot. There'd be no mid-day lunch this Sunday, as it was the one Sunday per month when the reverend drove to the nearby field camp to deliver a second sermon to the orchard workers. A mission shared equally by the four local houses of worship.

With no scheduled after-church event, Chloe realized she and Jessi could make a quick escape once the adult services were over and the parents came to claim their children. As much as she hated working on the weekends, and taking time away from her daughter, she needed to put in a few hours at the co-op offices rearranging the banners and replacing the flyers with the new month's sale offers.

Part of her marketing strategy included revolving sales of produce, usually a month behind the harvest. So, the oranges picked last month that hadn't sold, would become this month's featured item. Next month, it will be lemons. Then, with any luck, the following month would feature the first harvest of avocados.

Then, once she'd finished, she and Jessi could spend the rest of their day together enjoying their new backyard gym set and cooking burgers on the huge grill her father had insisted on installing on her deck.

Drew shifted in the front seat of his car and faced his uncle. "So, where to go first? Do you want to get some lunch at Steph's Place?"

"Maybe after we go by the co-op," Sam commented. "Let the other church goers get in and out of the diner first so it won't be so danged crowded."

"Sounds good." Pulling out onto the main road, he waved his hand toward town and announced loudly, "To the co-op."

At his side, Sam stifled an outright laugh.

When they arrived, the first thing Drew noticed was the compact SUV he'd seen earlier in the church parking lot. Given the co-op was closed on Sunday's it was likely the woman was an employee, rather than a customer. And, if so, Sam would know her.

No doubt, an introduction was eminent. The thought pleased him.

Sam led the way to the back door, fishing for his keys in his jacket pocket as he walked. "Shouldn't be anybody here today." Giving a sharp nod toward the other car, he grumbled, "'cept *her*, I guess."

Drew followed his uncle inside the dimly lit building. The smell of fresh produce filled the air. Bins of apples, oranges, lemons, and pears sat center court, surrounded by tables loaded with vine fruits. To the side, a display of avocados took up very little space. With only two growers in the immediate area, Sam and his best friend Jake Patterson were small potatoes compared to the citrus and apple orchards.

Shelves lined the walls with locally canned goods. One wall had been devoted to at least six different brands of honey, both regular and specialty.

A light shone from the corner manager's office, and the two men made their way in that direction. They'd almost reached the doorway when a young girl came out of the room, stopping just short of where they stood.

She raised her head and stared straight at Drew. "I know Mr. Morgan, but who are you?"

He did his best to hide his grin. "I'm Drew. Who are you?"

"Jessi," she responded, her chocolate gaze narrowing with suspicion. "My mom works here."

Sam's attention went from the young girl, to him, and back again. "I wasn't expecting to see anyone here on Sunday."

"We're putting up the new posters," a husky, but decidedly feminine, voice said from the office door. "I wasn't expecting to see anyone either."

"Just giving my nephew a tour."

Drew shifted his stance and met the woman's gaze. She was even more beautiful up close. He stuck out his hand. "Hi, I'm Drew Morgan."

She placed her hand in his, her grip firmer than he expected.

"Chloe Taylor, and you've already met my daughter Jessi."

The marketing manager. And she has a daughter. His previous enthusiasm plummeted. A daughter likely meant the knock-out brunette also had a husband.

"It's nice to meet you, Chloe Taylor," Drew said, pulling back his hand.

"No, it's not," Sam insisted. "This is the upstart woman trying to get me to sign onto her fancy marketing plan."

Chloe Taylor's brown eyes, a shade darker than her daughter's, rolled around in obvious exasperation. "Perhaps, Mr. Morgan, if you'd just give my plan a chance—"

"Nope." Waving his hand to encompass the main floor of the cooperative, Sam nodded toward the corner display. "Not until you give my crops the same fancy attention those orange and apple growers get."

Drew waited patiently to see how this 'upstart woman' would respond.

"If you'd bothered reading my plan," she said calmly, "you'd realize that the rotation of featured produce depends on crop yield. Once we get to the end of April, when you and Mr. Patterson have brought in your first full harvests, you'll both get a proportional amount of space."

"Yet, them danged hippies and their fancy honey get an entire wall," Sam groused. "When I was coming up, this entire area was nothing but avocado farms. Now, there's just the two of us left."

Chloe pressed her fists to her slender hips, the defiant motion drawing Drew's chuckle. Perhaps Sam's housekeeper wasn't the only woman willing to stand up to him.

"And nobody knows you're here," she said, her voice still calm. Even. "Because you refuse to market your product properly."

"She has a point," Drew put in, his agreement drawing Sam's angry glare. "I'm just saying, the website looks good. Even you agreed with that. Mrs. Taylor obviously knows her stuff."

"It's Miss Taylor," she corrected.

Drew's pulse picked up speed. *No husband.* Score!

"Why don't we sit down tomorrow, as planned, at eleven," Chloe suggested. "The three of us can go over everything in detail."

"Andrew's only here for a few months," Sam pointed out. "He's military and he's got more important places to be than here with me. So, it's my decision, not his."

"You're right, of course," she agreed. "However,

a third opinion never hurts."

"Fine," Sam conceded. "We'll listen to your proposal. But I'm not making any promises."

Chloe smiled sweetly and gave a nod of her head, the simple motion sending her long hair flying across her shoulders, ratcheting up Drew's pulse a full notch.

Chapter Three

"Are we going home now?" Jessi asked.

"Yes, sweetie, we are. Thank you for your help today."

"It was fun. And, really nice of Mr. Morgan's nephew to hang those big posters for us. He didn't even need a ladder. He's really tall."

Tall, handsome, and built. Her heart still raced with the memory of Drew Morgan stretching up to tack the posters in place. The way his dress pants clung to his...

Chloe drew a breath and blew it out in an effort to calm herself.

Shame he's only here for a few months.

A shame, yes. Yet, it was for the best. The last thing she needed was a distraction. Even one as drop-dead sexy as Andrew Morgan.

Building her career, and a life for herself and Jessi, were her first objectives. Her only objectives, at the moment. Moving her business from Fresno, where firms like hers were a dime a dozen, to the smaller rural area surrounding Plentiful was a risk, but one she was willing to take if it meant a stable home for her daughter. And a chance to escape the errors of her past.

"Can we stop for milkshakes at the diner?"

Jessi's hopeful smile tugged on her maternal heartstrings. "We'll see, sweetie."

They were on the road home within a few minutes and Chloe had every intention of granting Jessi's request. That was until she noticed Sam and Drew Morgan going up the stairs and into the diner. The last thing she wanted was for the two men to think she was following them.

"It looks pretty crowded in there," she commented off-handedly. "How about instead of milkshakes, I make us some floats? We have vanilla bean ice cream, and I'm pretty sure there's orange soda."

"Burgers and floats. Hmm..." Jessi said with a wide grin. "And chocolate chip cookies for dessert?"

"Don't press your luck," Chloe teased. "We'll make a fruit salad for dessert."

"Fine," Jessi responded with a sigh. "As long as there's cheese on the burgers."

Chloe's laugh echoed through the car. "Always. A burger's not a burger without cheese."

Monday morning dawned overcast and cooler than usual. A light drizzle fell.

Chloe dropped her daughter off at school, kept her nine o'clock appointment, and now sat in her SUV on the side of the road. Once she filed away Abel Patterson's signed contract, it would be time to make the twenty-five-mile drive to Plenty Good Farms.

The last hurdle in her plan.

At fifteen minutes to eleven, she pulled onto Sam Morgan's property and stopped in the circle drive. She was about to exit the car when Drew came around the side of the house, his arms filled with branch scraps.

He was dressed in a pair of beige combat pants and an extremely snug fitting, olive-green t-shirt. The shirt was damp from the light rain and clung to his chest, accentuating his well-toned muscles. His very appearance made Chloe's throat go as dry as the nearby fields in the heat of summer.

He stopped at her passenger door and, when she rolled down the window, he poked his head inside.

"Welcome. My uncle's waiting—somewhat impatiently—in the kitchen."

"But, I'm early—"

Drew's deep chuckle reverberated through her entire body.

"Early to Sam would have been before dawn. He's itching to get out in the fields and check on the newest trees."

"Well, then," she said firmly, opening her car door as she spoke. "Let's get this meeting started."

He tossed the dead branches on a pile beside the porch and motioned her forward. "Word of warning—if he offers you coffee—accept."

"Why?"

"Sam doesn't trust anyone who doesn't drink coffee."

She gave a sound shake of her head and followed Drew up the front stairs. "I don't think your uncle trusts anyone. And, especially, not me."

"Why don't you head down to the kitchen, while I make a pit stop to change my shirt? I'll only be a minute."

She made her way along a narrow hallway, the walls adorned with pictures from years past. She stopped for a moment to admire a family portrait. Sam, a very lovely woman, and a young boy. Drew, perhaps? If the talk going around town was accurate, Sam and his late wife had never had children of their own, but had raised Drew from an early age. Sparing one last glance at the photo, she continued on.

The enormous kitchen caught her off guard. She

wasn't sure what she was expecting, but it certainly wasn't this warm and decidedly family-oriented room. Chintz curtains framed three large windows that overlooked the backyard, an oversized stove took up one-half of the farthest wall and, in the middle of it all, sat a beautifully carved table big enough to seat twelve.

Sam sat at one end of the table. His hands were wrapped tightly around a huge mug.

Chloe took a seat at the opposite end and sat her briefcase on the floor at her feet. When she looked up, Drew was standing in the doorway, a fresh t-shirt in place.

"Get the lady a cup of coffee, Andrew," Sam suggested, his gaze pinning her to the chair.

Chloe looked up and met Drew's broad grin. "Yes, please. I'd love a cup. Black is fine."

The corner of Drew's mouth twitched. "Black? Really? I'd have pictured you for a cream and sugar woman."

"Well, then, you're not picturing me correctly, at all. Are you?"

Across the table, Sam snickered. "You heard her, boy. Get her that coffee."

"Yes, sir. Right away." Drew poured the coffee and placed the cup in front of her, leaning close to whisper, "Good luck. Sam's coffee's been known to grow hairs on a man's chest."

Chloe offered both men her sweetest smile and lifted the cup to her lips, pulling in a mouthful of hot coffee. Thick as mud, bitter to the tongue, she swallowed it back. "Delicious."

Sam's gaze narrowed, as if he didn't believe her. So, to prove she wasn't about to be intimidated, she took another healthy swig before setting the cup aside.

"You brought all your paperwork," Sam stated.

"Yes, I did." She retrieved the folder and laid it on the table. "I know you're still a bit hesitant, but I'm willing to cut you a deal to bring you onboard."

"What kind of deal?" Sam asked, suspicion lacing his question.

"Most of the farms are in for two-years. Abel Patterson signed for one year. I'm willing to give you a six-month contract, with the option to renew for another six or eighteen months. If I haven't proven valuable in increasing your business, you don't have to reup at all."

"Why the special treatment?" Drew questioned. "Surely you could go ahead with your plans even if Sam didn't sign on at all."

"Yes, I could," she admitted. "However, part of my strategy includes an aerial tour of the member orchards. It wouldn't do to have a gaping hole in the video, now would it?"

"And just what is this deal going to cost me?"

"The monthly charge is one-hundred dollars per farm, if you sign on for a year or two. Ordinarily, it would be more for a shorter contract. But, again, I'm willing to cut a deal."

Chloe took another sip of her coffee, her gaze intent on Sam's. In the periphery of her vision, she could see Drew thumbing through the contract she'd laid on the table.

"Can I ask you a question?" The resonant tone of Drew's voice pulled her gaze to his.

"Yes, of course. That's why I'm here. To answer your questions."

"I've read the background information on your business website. You worked for a marketing firm in Fresno that specialized in wineries. After that, you went into business for yourself and worked mostly with grocery chains."

"That's correct," she said, wondering where he was going. And when his question would come.

"What do you know about fruit orchards? Avocados, especially."

"Good question, Andrew," Sam added. "Yes, young lady, what *do* you know?"

"I've done my homework. I understand crop yields, harvesting schedules and methods. I know how long a certain fruit will last, off the tree, before it's past its prime." Staring directly at Sam, she continued. "I know avocados have one of the shortest lifespans once they're harvested. At least fresh avocados. Now that companies are freezing them—"

Sam's shudder stopped her mid-sentence. "I know it's a new business, at least for consumers, but it ruins a perfectly good piece of God's bounty."

Chloe pressed her fingers to her lips to hold in her laugh. "I've no doubt that a fresh avocado is far superior to a frozen one. However, if freezing extends the value of your product and keeps you from disposing of unsold crops, it's got to be considered a viable option."

"Up until a year or so ago, my crops were sold out. Whatever goes on at the other end, after they're bought, is of no matter to me."

"What happened to change your sell-through?" Chloe asked. She knew the answer, but wondered if Sam would be upfront about the reasons.

"Drought," he mumbled. "Out of date irrigation equipment. My own fault," he admitted. "My customers had to go elsewhere. Some didn't come back."

"You never told me that, Sam," Drew said, his gaze intent on his uncle. "Why didn't you say something?"

"There wasn't anything you could do thousands of miles away."

"Well, I intend to make it my job," Chloe explained, "to ensure we not only get those customers back, but add some new ones as well."

Sam reached for the contract in front of Drew. "I'll give you a year. If you can do as you say, I'll reup for a second year." He withdrew a pen from his shirt pocket and asked, "Where do I sign?"

"Wait!" Drew said suddenly. "Shouldn't we talk about this? Just the two of us?"

Chloe's breath caught. Why was Drew throwing a wrench into her plans, when his uncle had finally come around?

Sam laid his pen down and turned toward his nephew. "I thought you said it looked like she knew her stuff?

"I'm not saying she doesn't," Drew explained. "I just think a year is a long time, given you're not getting any younger."

"What's that supposed to mean?"

Drew released a long sigh and turned to Chloe. "Can you give us an extra day to talk things over? I've no doubt your services are worth what you're charging, but my uncle and I need to discuss a few other things before he signs."

"Fine, of course" she responded, although she felt anything but fine. "How about I come back tomorrow afternoon?"

"I can bring the paperwork to you, rather than have you drive back out here," Drew offered.

Chloe met his gaze and shook her head. "That's okay. I've got to come in this direction anyway to grab a few photos of Harlan's peach orchard. Then, assuming Sam does sign, I'll want to take some of your avocado fields as well." She paused, then asked, "Is one o'clock okay?"

"Yes," both Sam and Drew said in unison.

Chloe pushed herself to her feet. "Thank you for the coffee, Sam. I'll see you both tomorrow at one."

Chapter Four

Drew watched from the porch as Chloe Taylor climbed into her car and drove away. He was not looking forward to the coming conversation with his uncle, but it had to happen. It should have happened when he first got here, but he'd not known how to broach the subject. Now, he had no choice.

"What was that all about?" Sam asked when Drew returned to the kitchen. "I thought you wanted me to sign up for her services."

"I think her plan is solid, and just what you need in the long run. First though, I think we need to have a serious conversation about your ability to keep working this farm with the skeleton staff of workers you've got at the moment."

"You're here now," Sam argued. "You'll get that scraggly bunch working full steam. And, once the first crops come in, we can hire another two or three pickers."

"I'm only here for a few months. Remember?" Drew pushed his fingers through his hair, the strands only slightly longer than his usual military cut. "You're sixty-eight, Sam. That's way too old to be working out in the fields day and night."

"I'm fine," Sam argued. "I can still outwork half my men."

"Only because you're too stubborn to admit you're hurting. I've seen those winces when you move the wrong way. The way your hands tremble."

"Nothing a bit of ointment won't cure. As for the tremble, I could do to cut back on my coffee a bit."

"I've talked to the doctor, Sam. I know you've got some issues."

"Danged big mouth. Whatever happened to patient confidentiality?"

"It was your idea to give me your power of attorney, for both business and your health decisions."

"Yeah, but you're only supposed to use them if I'm incapacitated. Not to gang up on me."

"The doc suggested it was time for you to retire. Or, at the very least, cut back."

"Not going to happen. I intend to work in my fields until the Almighty decides otherwise."

"That's just it, old man. You'll likely die on your tractor."

Sam's weathered gaze darkened, but his smile lifted. "I can't think of a better way to go."

"I'd much rather you live another twenty or thirty years in comfort."

"And just how do you propose I do that?" Sam asked.

Drew had no doubt, Sam wasn't going to like his answer. "Sell this place. Retire. You've got more than enough money to live on."

"This is home, Andrew. Where else would I go?"

"You could buy a smaller place in town. Or, maybe, come live with me? I've got a place off-base. It's not huge, like this house, but it's plenty big enough for the two of us."

"The two of us?" Sam gave a deep sigh. "What happens when you finally decide to settle down with a wife? A family? You won't want an old man hanging around then."

"Who says I ever intend to settle down? The military has been my life for a long time now. I'm not sure I'm suited to a wife and family."

"Don't be a fool, Andrew. The happiest years of my life were when your aunt was alive, when we were raising you."

Drew closed his eyes and let Sam's words—the memories—sink in. Yes, those were good times. The work was hard, the summers scorching hot, the days long. Yet, when they came in from the fields, Aunt Harriet was there, a home cooked meal on the table.

A pie or cookies for dessert. And, all the love a man and a boy could handle.

"I really miss her," Drew admitted, pushing away a single tear from the corner of his eye.

"Me too, Andrew. Me too."

"One thing I do know, Aunt Harriet wouldn't have wanted you to work yourself to the bone like this. She'd be right here with me, telling you to cut back."

"I'll tell you what," Sam said. "How about we see how your medical leave goes? If you get the all clear and can go back to work, we'll look at me cutting back. Maybe adding on a permanent farm manager. If you can't go back to work, you've got a job here with me. I've no intention of selling this place. Never have, never will."

"But—" How could he tell the man who meant the world to him that he didn't want to be an avocado farmer? Especially when—financially—there was no need to be.

"Once I'm gone, it's yours to do with as you please. Keep it or sell it. But, this is where I'm spending my last years, good or bad."

The next afternoon, Drew was unloading the supplies he'd picked up in town when Chloe Taylor pulled into the driveway and parked behind him.

When she exited her SUV, Drew stopped what he was doing and met her at the porch steps.

"I'm sorry about yesterday," he told her. "I don't want you to think I was trying to talk Sam out of signing the contract. He and I had a few other things to discuss."

"Is he okay?" she asked, her tone sincere. "Rumor going around town is that he's not well."

"That's all it is... a rumor. He's got a few minor problems, not unusual for a man in his late sixties. However, he's not going anywhere for a while."

"That's good to hear."

"Not that I'd mind if he retired and sold this place," Drew admitted. "But that's never going to happen."

"So, you're not chomping at the bit to take over for him when you get out of the military?"

"Not me. I don't know yet what I'll do when I leave the military, but I'm pretty sure it won't be working on an avocado farm. I did enough of that as a boy."

"That's right, you grew up here on the farm, didn't you?"

He shot her a narrowed stare. "I see the good people of Plentiful have been talking."

"Your sudden return, after... what... a half-dozen years set tongues wagging."

"It's only been four years," he corrected. "The gossips should get their stories straight."

She laughed softly, the lilt in her voice pulling out a return smile.

"What do you do in the military?"

"I protect people. Specifically, the engineers and crew who rebuild the bridges destroyed by conflict," he told her. "I got my degree in criminal justice from UCLA. After graduation, I enlisted and became part of the advance forces for the military corp of engineers. My earliest duties consisted of making sure the area we were going into was secure, so my on-the-job training took place all over the world."

"Sounds like an important job," she commented. "You said 'earliest duties', what about now?"

Before he could respond, the front door opened. Sam stood on the threshold.

"You two coming in? Or are we doing business on the porch?"

"We're coming in," Chloe confirmed. "Hopefully, you've got some coffee ready."

Sam's grin spread. "There's always a pot on the stove when I'm not out in the fields. Come on back to the kitchen and sit down. I'll get you a cup."

Drew closed the distance between himself and Chloe. Leaning close, he whispered, "I guess I've been replaced as the coffee lackey."

"Shame," she teased. "You were getting so good at it."

Once the contract was signed, Chloe gathered up the papers and put them in her briefcase. "Would you mind if I wandered around a bit and took some pictures? I won't be long. I have to be home by three-thirty for Jessi's school bus."

"Andrew can take you out to the start of the fields if you'd like, get you closer to the crops," Sam offered.

"I don't want to impose. I'm sure I can get some great pictures without going all the way into the fields."

"I'm driving out anyway," Drew told her. "I've got to stake a few of the smaller trees. I can work while you wander around and take your photos."

"Why not? That way, I can get some shots coming from the field to the house."

"Who's doing your aerial photography?" Drew asked.

"I'm not sure yet," she admitted. "I've got to map out the route first. Then, I'll take bids. I've also got interest from two companies who film by drone."

"A drone would definitely get closer to the

ground."

"I don't want none of those nosey things flying over my crops," Sam put in. Turning to Drew, he suggested, "Why don't you take Chloe up in the plane and let her decide on the route she wants the photographers to take?"

Chloe looked from Drew to Sam and back again. "You're a pilot?"

"Small planes," Drew confirmed. "Nothing bigger than Sam's Cessna."

She turned back to Sam. "You fly too?"

"Naw, not me. The plane belonged to my late wife. She was the pilot. Harriet was the one who taught Drew. I could have sold the danged thing, I suppose, but I thought Drew might want it someday."

She pulled in a silent breath. The Morgan men were certainly surprising her.

"Well, if you're ready, we can head up the hill," Drew said, drawing Chloe from her thoughts.

"Yes, of course. Just let me grab my camera from the car."

Once they were in Drew's four-wheel drive and headed up the dirt road toward the start of the orchard, he asked, "What brought you here to Plentiful?"

"It's a funny story, really. A couple of friends

and I were driving south from Fresno to Mexico for the weekend. We got off the highway for gas and the first station was closed, so we came a little farther down the road and ended up on the outskirts of town. We passed a number of small businesses, the whitewashed co-op building, and the Saturday flea market, before we finally reached the one open gas station."

"Ah, yes, our one-horse town."

"One of a half dozen small towns in the county. Anyway, while we were gassing up, I started a conversation with the clerk. He mentioned that they used to run a farmer's market every weekend, but when the state rerouted the highway, business dropped to the point that they ended up turning the farmer's market into a flea market."

"I remember the original market," he commented. "It was packed all day Saturday and then again on Sunday afternoon after church services."

"When I got back to Fresno, I did a little research on the area, only to discover the orchards around here are some of the biggest producers of nearly every type of fruit grown in the state. And, while they still ship throughout the state, very few people actually come to the area other than those who live or vacation here."

"That's when you decided to move here and save our little community with modern marketing ideas?"

"I'd started my own marketing firm, but competition was stiff at home, so I thought... why not? I packed everything into a moving truck, pulled Jessi out of school, and headed south. My parents came along to help us get settled. I'd found a house to rent online." Chuckling softly, she added, "My dad even insisted on installing a barbeque on the deck."

"Um... what about Jessi's dad? He didn't mind you taking her away?"

"Jessi's dad hasn't been in the picture since I first found out I was expecting."

"Sorry," he apologized.

"Don't be. It wasn't your fault. I'm the one who trusted the wrong man, fell for his line of undying love, married him without really knowing him, and watched him walk away the moment I told him I was pregnant."

"That's rough."

"I was young, stupid. Thankfully, my parents were understanding and helped me obtain a quick divorce that was final before Jessi was born. Between them and my faith, I was able to recover quickly. Part of that recovery was to return to using my family name. When Jessi was born, I chose to give her my last name as well. She was never going to know her father, so there was no reason not to."

"She's a cutie pie, and very polite."

"Yes, she is. What about you? Ever married? Children?"

"Nope. Like I said earlier, I went straight from college to the military. I've spent the better part of twelve years in a half-dozen foreign countries. I've had no time, or inclination, to find a wife or start a family."

Drew pulled to a halt beside a narrow road leading into the fields. Once they'd left the car, she told him, "I'll get started on my pictures and meet you back here at the car. How long will you be?"

"I should be done in thirty minutes, maybe less."

"Sounds good. That'll give me plenty of time to get some close up and long-range shots and still make it home in plenty of time for Jessi."

Avocado Toast by Nancy Fraser

Chapter Five

Drew let himself into the farmhouse after walking Chloe to her car. She was not what he was expecting. True, she was ambitious, a hard worker intent on succeeding. But, she also had a vulnerable side to her. Her concern over Sam's health was touching. As was her admission to having faith.

Having spent so many years in places where his Christian religion was not practiced, he knew better than anyone the power of faith. His belief in God helped him through many perilous situations.

"The clinic called," Sam said when Drew walked into the kitchen. "They want you to come in tomorrow at ten for your first follow-up. I told them to expect you, unless you called back and let them know otherwise."

"That'll be fine. I'm anxious to get this whole forced leave behind me."

Drew couldn't miss the frown that briefly crossed Sam's face. While he knew his uncle would never wish him ill, Drew got the distinct impression

Sam hoped he'd stay on forever.

Like he'd told Chloe just a short time earlier, he didn't see his future including long days in the hot sun harvesting avocados. Yet, in the back of his head, Drew knew if push came to shove, he'd be hard pressed to desert the man who'd taken him in when his parents had died in a freak boating accident.

Sam and Harriet had raised him to believe in God, and follow the Golden Rule. When his aunt died four years earlier, it wasn't just Sam she'd left behind to grieve. Drew had been devastated.

"How long is the drive to the clinic?" Sam asked.

"About ninety-minutes each way," Drew responded absently. "I'll be back in the early afternoon." Drew snatched a bottle of soda from the fridge, and turned back to Sam. "Can I ask you a question?"

Sam shrugged, the width of his shoulders was not nearly as broad as Drew remembered.

"I 'spose so."

"It's about Chloe Taylor. She mentioned something to me earlier about relying on her faith, and I remember seeing her in the church parking lot on Sunday. Yet, she wasn't in services."

"Sunday School," Sam said simply. "She took over for Marilyn Porter last year. The kids really seem to like her."

"Something tells me, Sam, you like her too. Far more than you let on when I first got here."

Sam bent his head and studied the tablecloth. "She reminds me of your aunt. Independent. Stubborn. Bossy."

Drew bit back a laugh. "In other words, *strong*. Just like Aunt Harriet."

"She's doing a good job raising her daughter, too. Right polite too, that little one." Sam raised his head, his gray gaze alight with mischief, his lips twitching as if he was holding in a laugh. "Why the sudden interest in Chloe? I thought you weren't 'in the market' for a woman."

"I'm not," Drew returned firmly. "Especially given she's... um... 'bossy'. The last thing I need is someone else bossing me around while I'm here."

"Are you taking her up in the plane? If so, I'll need to have it checked and fueled."

"I made the offer, but she hasn't accepted. At least not yet. I even told her she could bring her daughter if she wanted."

"Probably a good idea," Sam agreed. "A chaperone will keep you from getting close. Since you're *not* interested."

Chloe stepped out onto her front porch and watched as Jessi hopped off the school bus, crossed the narrow road, and let herself in through the gate of the picket fence surrounding their yard.

"How was school?"

Jessi spun around in a circle, kicking up dust where the grass hadn't fully filled in. "It was great. I made the junior mixed soccer team."

"Junior team?"

"Grades one through three. So, boys and girls get to play together. Next year, I can try out for the girl's senior team."

"Sounds like fun."

"Did you get Mr. Morgan to sign his contract? Finally."

"Yes, he signed on for one year. I spent an hour or so taking pictures of his property. He's got a really nice view from the top of the hill leading to his orchard."

"You got to climb up a hill?" Jessi asked, obviously impressed with the idea of a hike.

"No, actually Drew—Mr. Morgan's nephew— drove me up in his four-wheel drive. He had some trees to take care of, so I wandered around while he worked." Chloe opened the door and ushered Jessi inside. Hesitantly, she explained, "Drew also offered to take me flying in Sam's plane. That way I can get a general idea of where I want the aerial photographers to shoot their film."

"A plane? Really?" Jessi's eyes lit with excitement.

"He invited you to come along," Chloe told her. "Assuming you want to, of course."

"Do I? You betcha. Can we, please? The kids at school will be so jealous."

Chloe shot her daughter a narrowed stare. "That doesn't seem like a very nice thing to do... purposely trying to make your friends jealous."

"They do it all the time," Jessi argued. "Patty Springer is always bragging about her new clothes, and—"

"That doesn't mean it's the right thing to do." When Jessi's smile faded, Chloe added, "There's nothing wrong with sharing your adventure with your friends, but not in a way that will make them feel bad about not having the same opportunity."

"Yes, ma'am. I understand."

"Why don't you get started on your homework? I'll cut up some apple and carrot sticks, and bring them to you in a couple of minutes."

"I don't have much to do. Just an extra credit set

of math problems and I have to finish my paragraph about my favorite insect."

"Do you have a favorite insect?"

"Not really, but I'm writing about lightning bugs because they're really cool."

Late the next morning, Chloe dialed the number for Sam Morgan's place. The phone rang three times before an out-of-breath female picked up.

"Morgan residence. This is Helen."

Sam's housekeeper. According to the town scuttlebutt, the only one who'd managed to stay longer than six months.

"Good morning, Helen. This is Chloe Taylor. Is Drew there?"

"Andrew? No, he's not. Not that I'd know for sure, since I haven't met the man yet. Sam said something about him leaving an hour before I got here."

"Leaving? Permanently?"

"No. He'll be back later today. He had to drive to San Diego for something."

Chloe released the breath she hadn't realized she'd drawn. Relief flooded through her.

Get a grip, girl. You just met the man.

"Is Sam available?" Chloe asked.

"He mumbled something about a storm coming

and needing to finish staking the smaller trees. Then, he took off on the tractor toward the fields." She huffed a breath. "Stubborn old coot. He should have just waited for his nephew to come back."

"He's definitely stubborn," Chloe agreed. "However, I'm sure he'll be fine. He's been doing this forever."

"I can have Sam call you when he gets back? Or, Andrew, if he gets here first?"

"That would be great, thank you. Sam has my number."

Chloe laid her cell down on the table with the intention of pouring herself another cup of coffee. Yet, rather than turn toward the kitchen, she grabbed her purse, phone, and car keys and headed for the door.

An uneasy feeling came over her. As if she was needed elsewhere. She wasn't sure why, or how, but knew she wouldn't relax until she'd checked on Sam.

By the time she reached Plenty Good Farms, the sky was dark. Rain fell in sheets, soaking the ground. Climbing out of the car, she made a dash for the back door rather than the front.

Helen answered immediately. Before the housekeeper said anything, Chloe asked, "Has Sam come back yet?"

"No," Helen responded. "I'm starting to get

worried."

"My car will make it up the hill," Chloe told her. "I'm going to check on him."

"I'd appreciate it if you would. I'd go with you, but should probably wait here for Andrew. If he gets home before you come back, I'll let him know where you've gone."

"Good thinking. I've got my cell with me. I'll call if I need help."

Drew turned off the highway at the exit closest to the farm. The drive back from San Diego had been nasty, the rain falling so hard even his heavy-duty wipers couldn't completely clear the windshield.

Negotiating the final turn in the road, the first thing he saw was the flashing red lights of the county sheriff's car in the driveway just beyond the gate. He pressed the accelerator down and the car surged forward.

He jumped out the moment the car came to a stop, barely taking the time to set the gears. "What's happened?"

A middle-aged woman Drew assumed to be Helen stood on the back porch, Chloe huddled close to the woman's side.

"It's Sam," Chloe said quickly. "There was an accident. He went out to finish anchoring the trees and the wind knocked one down, pinning him beneath it."

"Where is he?"

"The ambulance left a few minutes ago," Helen said. "I didn't have your cell number, or I would have called. Thankfully, Chloe found him and called for help."

"That's okay, Helen. Now that I'm here, I'll head into town and meet them at the clinic."

"I'll go with you," Chloe offered.

Drew nodded. "I'd appreciate it." Once they were seated in his car, Drew backed out onto the road, and then asked, "How did you happen to be here?"

"I'd called earlier to accept your offer of a plane ride. Helen said Sam had gone up the hill." She pulled in an audible breath. "I can't explain it, but I got this queasy feeling in the pit of my stomach. I got the sense I had to drive over and check on him."

"It sounds like it's a good thing that you did. Thank you."

"The EMT thinks he has a sprained ankle and maybe a cracked rib or two. Of course, Sam was insisting he was fine."

"Stubborn old man," Drew grumbled. "How did you get the tree off of him?"

"I didn't. I tried, but couldn't lift it. That's when I called the sheriff. He and his deputy were able to raise the branches far enough so the EMTs could pull Sam out." She reached across the width of his four-wheeler and laid her hand on his arm. "It was the weirdest thing I've ever seen. His injuries could have—should have—been much worse given the size of the tree. It was like the longer branches made a cocoon around him, sheltering him from the heavier trunk of the tree."

"Saved by the trees he loves so much. And, no doubt, by the grace of the Almighty."

"Amen," Chloe whispered.

"Amen, indeed."

Chapter Six

While he skirted the speed limit driving to the Plentiful Medical Clinic, Chloe called her neighbor and asked if she'd watch for Jessi's bus. "The advantages of a small town," Chloe said when she disconnected her call. "Everyone's willing to do for others when necessary."

"I'd say I was surprised that she didn't ask why you needed her help, but—like you said—small town. No doubt the news of Sam's accident got here before the ambulance. As well as the fact you were the one who called it in."

"No doubt," she agreed. "I'm just glad you made it back when you did."

Drew blew out a long breath. "Yeah, I'd have been earlier but the weather slowed me down. Not to mention my own brand of Morgan stubbornness."

"You? Stubborn? Where could you possibly have learned that behavior?"

"Sam's got nothing on me when I'm angry."

Her fingers flexed where they lay against his

arm, and she asked, "Anything I can do to help?"

"No, but thank you. Fighting with the army's medical experts is something I have to do on my own."

"I take it you don't agree with their assessment."

"According to the *specialist* in San Diego, I never should have been given the option of a three-month leave with the possibility of returning to active duty."

"Why not? You seem perfectly healthy to me, other than a slight limp when you walk."

He shot a quick glance across the width of the car. "You've watched me walk?"

"Don't go getting all full of yourself, Drew. I only noticed because I was walking behind you when you led the way up the hill to the orchard."

"Well, that's a shame," he teased. "Because I've definitely watched you walk. There's an enticing sway to your hips."

"Perhaps, but I'm not the one who has to deal with physio and specialists."

"True enough." He pulled into the parking spot closest to the clinic door. "Which was what brought out my stubborn streak."

Once they were on their way into the clinic, Chloe responded. "Angry I can understand, but why stubborn?"

"Rather than leave the clinic right away, I made a point of calling my C.O. back on base. I wasted a good thirty minutes listening to him tell me how—if he had his way—I'd be shipped out tomorrow. Then, in the end, admitting he had no control over the final decision." Drew slammed his closed fist against the hallway wall as they walked, not hard enough to damage anything, but just enough to underscore his next point. "Perhaps, if I'd left right away instead of sulking, I would have missed the worst of the weather and been here in time to prevent Sam's accident."

"Or, you'd have been up there working at his side and it would have been you the tree fell on," she reasoned. Flashing him a mocking grin, she told him, "Either way, I'd still be here, smelling the horrible antiseptic stench of the clinic."

"Aww, poor Chloe," he teased. "No limp, or sprained ankle, or possibly broken ribs."

The next morning, Chloe took a seat off to the side of Sam's hospital bed, leaving Drew to take the one closest to where his uncle slept. She watched intently, as the younger man studied his uncle's features. The gentle way he stroked the back of

Sam's hand sent a lump to her throat.

"You know," Drew said quietly. "He's going to be a bear and a half when the sedative they gave him wears off."

"Thankfully, I don't have to live with him."

"Maybe not, but I do, so you could feel a bit of compassion for me too."

Oh, you feel something all right. Far more than compassion.

Pushing aside the taunt of her overzealous conscience, she rushed to assure him. "I'll do my best."

"Assuming they let Sam out of here tomorrow as planned, do you still want to go up for a bird's eye view of the county on Saturday morning?" Drew asked.

"Won't you be needed at home?"

"I can have Helen come over and keep him company. Now that I've actually met the woman, I can understand why they get along. She obviously doesn't take any of his guff."

"If you're sure, I suppose we could go. I know Jessi's excited about the idea."

"Why don't you and Jessi come out to the house for breakfast around nine? I make a mean frittata."

"That sounds great. What can I bring?"

He shook his head. "Nothing. I've got everything

covered. I'll even throw in some fresh-squeezed orange juice from Sam's private grove."

"Oranges on an avocado farm? The travesty!"

"Shh... don't tell anyone. They were my aunt's prized possessions. Two Meyer lemon trees, two Washington navels, and one Valencia."

"Your aunt sounds like a remarkable woman. A loving wife, caring aunt, pilot, and citrus tree owner. Despite being surrounded by avocados."

"She was definitely my best influence growing up. I may have gotten my stubborn streak from Sam, but I got my patience and empathy from her."

"And your faith?" Chloe asked.

"That came from them both, thankfully. I don't remember a Sunday growing up that the three of us weren't glued to Sam's favorite pew."

"Perhaps you can draw on some of that faith now, both for yourself and for Sam's recovery."

"Whatcha two gabberin' about?" Sam asked, barely conscious but doing his best to roust himself into a seated position.

"Take it easy, Sam," Drew warned. "I'll crank the head of the bed up a bit."

Chloe rose to her feet and reached for the glass of water on the bedside table. "Would you like a drink?"

Sam cautiously took a sip. "Thank you." After

taking a second pull on the straw, he asked, "So, what were you two talking about? You'd better not be planning on leaving me here any longer than necessary."

"Quite the contrary," Drew told him. "We were just discussing your at-home recuperation."

"Won't take long," Sam insisted. "I'll be up and moving before you know it."

"I've no doubt of that," Drew agreed. "However, you *will* follow the doctor's orders. I'll see to it."

"Hmph... so you think," Sam grumbled before turning in Chloe's direction. "I suppose I owe you an extra 'thank you' for showing up when you did."

"You already thanked me," she reminded him. "Twice, in fact. Right after you cussed me out for coming up the hill in the middle of the storm."

"Well, I am thankful," Sam repeated.

"I'm just glad I got there when I did. The branches were protecting you from the brunt of the tree's weight but, with the rain coming down, that wasn't going to last long."

"The sheriff had his deputies put the tree to the side," Drew explained. "I'll go out later today and see if there's anything that can be salvaged. Maybe we can root some new saplings."

"Don't go fussing over it. We got plenty more trees to worry about."

It was nearly two when Chloe arrived at the house. She had some work to do before Jessi got home from school. Perhaps, after Jessi finished her homework, they'd go to the café for dinner. Given her daughter's love of their signature mac and cheese, there was no doubt she'd be as eager to go out, as Chloe was to not have to cook.

She was about to open her laptop and get to work when her cell rang.

"Good afternoon, Taylor Marketing, Chloe speaking."

"Hello, Chloe speaking." Drew's deep voice wrapped around his teasing words.

"Didn't I just leave you an hour or so ago? Seems to me you should be four games of checkers deep by now."

"Sam threw me out," he explained. "Apparently, he was tired of my hovering. I think he wanted to take another nap."

"Not that he would admit to it."

Drew's laugh tickled her senses.

"You got that right." He cleared his throat, and asked, "I don't suppose I could treat you and Jessi to dinner tonight? As a thank you for helping Sam."

"It's not necessary. I'm happy he's—"

"Well then, how about I take you to dinner

because I want to? Nothing to do with Sam. We won't even mention his name."

"Are you asking me—and my eight-year-old daughter—on a date?"

"Technically, it wouldn't be a date if Jessi's with us. Unless, of course, you'd like to get a sitter and make it a date."

"How about we meet at Steph's Place at six? The three of us."

"So... no date?"

"Not tonight anyway."

"Sounds promising," he admitted. "Like I told you, I got my patience from my Aunt Harriet, and that woman was a saint."

Chapter Seven

Drew couldn't remember the last time he was this nervous over something as simple as sharing a meal at Plentiful's local diner. Given it wasn't a 'real date', he'd settled on jeans and a t-shirt. He'd wrestled with whether to shave again, or just go with his afternoon scruff. His six o'clock shadow won out.

Chloe's car was in the parking lot when he arrived at Steph's Place so he took the spot next to hers and jogged up the stairs to the front entrance. The moment he stepped through the door he saw Jessi waving to him from the corner booth.

"Good evening, ladies," he greeted before sliding onto the open bench.

"Good evening, Drew," Chloe said in return. "How's Sam doing?"

"I stopped in to check on him when I got back to town. As expected, he's driving the two afternoon nurses crazy. He keeps insisting he's well enough to go home on his own. Thankfully, the doc wrote orders to release him in the morning."

"I'm glad Mr. Morgan is better," Jessi said.

"Thank you, Jessi."

"My mom says you're taking us flying Saturday morning."

"That's right. I am. Are you excited about going up in a plane?"

"Yes, but I promised I wouldn't brag about it at school. I don't want to make my classmates jealous." She paused, then asked, "Can Boomer come with us?"

"Who's Boomer?"

"Our dog," Chloe informed him. Turning to Jessi, she added, "And, no, Boomer can't come along."

"But, mom—"

"Your mom's right," Drew jumped in, defending Chloe's parental decision. "Some animals don't tolerate flying very well. Especially in smaller planes."

The waitress arrived at that moment to drop off water and menus, her gingham checked uniform reminiscent of the café's retro theme. "Do you need time with menus, or do you already know what you want?"

"I want mac and cheese," Jessi said quickly. "Broccoli for my vegetable, and chocolate milk to drink."

Drew bit back a laugh. "I'll have the same, except ice tea to drink instead of chocolate milk." Turning to Chloe, he inquired, "And for you, ma'am?"

Chloe lifted the menus from the tabletop and handed them to their server. "I'll take a Stephburger with gouda, lettuce, tomato, and mayo. Plus, a side salad with ranch, and ice tea."

Once the woman had walked away, Jessi poked Drew on the hand to get his attention. "Exactly how *small* is your plane?"

"Have you ever seen a dragonfly?"

Jessi's gaze narrowed, her attention going from him to her mother and back, before she nodded. A look of panic furrowed the young girl's forehead.

"Well, it's bigger than that."

"Whew!" Chloe said, wiping her forearm across her brow in an exaggerated fashion. "You had me worried there for a minute."

Drew took his wallet from his back pocket and withdrew a worn picture from the side slot. "Here you go. She seats four with room for cargo." He laid the picture in front of Jessi and ran his fingertips over the image of the woman in the photo. "That's my Aunt Harriet. She's the one who taught me how to fly."

"Your aunt was a pilot?" Jessi questioned.

"That's so cool. I'd love to learn how to fly. Maybe you could teach me some day."

"Well, you've got a few years to think about it before you can get your training permit," Drew explained. "But, if I'm still here when you're old enough, and if it's okay with your mother, I'd be happy to give you lessons."

Their conversation circled from planes, to Jessi's first soccer outing, to Chloe's marketing plan.

"What breed is Boomer?" Drew asked when the conversation turned to the family pet.

"He's a Bagel Hound," Jessi told him. "His mother was a beagle, and his dad a basset hound."

When Chloe stifled her smile by biting her lower lip between her teeth, Drew's breath caught. She followed the enticing nibble with the quick stroke of her tongue, the simple gesture sending a distinct racing to his pulse.

The desire to repeat the caress of her lips with his own tongue turned the race up to full speed, the image of holding her in his arms filling his thoughts.

"I don't know that I've ever seen a Bagel Hound before," he admitted. "Does he eat bagels?"

Jessi gave a slow roll of her eyes before meeting his gaze. "Boomer eats *everything*."

"Including at least three of Jessi's school backpacks," Chloe added. "Although, he really only rips them open to get to the snacks inside. He doesn't actually eat the material or the zipper. Thank goodness."

"Boomer sounds like a character. Maybe I'll get to meet him someday."

"You could meet him when you come to our house to take mom out on a date." When both he and Chloe turned their attention to her, Jessi added, "If you ever decide to date her, I mean. You know... with kissing and stuff."

Drew burst into a loud laugh. Chloe, he noticed, struggled to keep from doing the same.

"And it would be okay with you if I ask your mother out on a date?"

"Sure." Jessi's grin spread. "That way, if you were boyfriend and girlfriend, we could go flying all the time."

"Yes," he agreed. "I guess we could."

At half-past eight, Drew let himself into the farmhouse. It had been one great evening. He couldn't remember ever having as much fun as he'd had with Chloe and Jessi. The idea of retirement didn't seem as daunting as it had, especially if it came with the prospect of staying on in Plentiful.

Even if it means you end up an avocado farmer?

Yes, even if.

Chloe set aside the night's chosen book once Jessi had finished reading her bedtime chapters. "Time for bed," she said firmly, assuming her daughter might try to negotiate more pages.

"Drew is really nice," Jessi commented as she was slipping between the sheets. "Do you like him?"

"Yes, of course. He's a very nice man."

"No, I mean... Do you *really* like him?"

"Like a boyfriend? With all the kissing and stuff?" Chloe teased.

"Yeah, like that."

"I don't know him that well. Besides, he may only be here for a few months. It wouldn't do to get too attached to someone who might leave."

"Like my dad did?"

Chloe's heart nearly stopped. "What did you just say? Whatever gave you the idea—"

"I overheard you and grandma talking when you were unpacking the boxes in your bedroom. She said it was good that we moved to get away from the memory of a failed marriage."

Sighing deeply, Chloe laid down beside her daughter and pulled Jessi to her side. "I guess this talk is coming a lot sooner than I'd expected."

"Why did you get divorced?"

"Our marriage wasn't working out, almost from the start. It just happened that I was expecting you when we separated."

"Does he live in Fresno?"

"No, sweetie. He left California and went back east to work for his father's law firm. I haven't heard from him since the divorce papers were signed. That was long before you were born."

"Could I meet him someday?"

"If you'd like, I'll contact him and see if he'd like to meet with you."

The shake of Jessi's head pressed into Chloe's shoulder.

"Maybe when I'm older," Jessi said. "I like it just the way it is now. Me, you, and Boomer. And maybe Drew, if he stays."

Avocado Toast by Nancy Fraser

Chapter Eight

Chloe double checked her tote bag and then put Boomer in his kennel. Saturday morning had dawned a bit overcast. Slowly, but surely, the sun was starting to peek through the clouds, holding promise for a perfect day.

Jessi was up by seven, a feat that never happened on school days. And, even though she'd answer at least a few dozen questions from her daughter the night before, Chloe was prepared for more this morning. Especially during the drive to Plenty Good Farms.

"Are you sure Drew won't change his mind about going because of his uncle?" Jessi asked.

"When he called last night he said Helen—their housekeeper—was going to be there by ten so we could leave. Mr. Morgan will be well looked after."

"But you were on the phone for so long," Jessi countered. "I was sure something was wrong."

"Nope, nothing wrong. We were just talking."

"About what?"

Chloe pulled in a long breath. Perhaps she could steer Jessi's questions back to airplanes and flight, as opposed to talking about hers and Drew's two-hour phone call.

"Actually, he was suggesting routes for our flight today and telling me about what it was like growing up on an avocado farm."

"I bet it was fun." Her eyes bright with excitement, Jessi gushed, "I'd love to live on a farm."

"Farming is hard work. You'd have chores early in the morning," she explained. "And after school." Chloe nudged her daughter toward the door and then set the alarm. "I'm not sure exactly what chores, since I've never actually lived on a farm, but I know there would be some, and they wouldn't always be easy. Just as the one chore you have each time we go out the door seems to have slipped your mind."

Jessi swung around. "No, it didn't. I stuck the sign up while you were putting Boomer in his kennel." She pointed to the corner of the picture window. "See."

Chloe spared a glance at the '*kenneled dog inside*' sign. "My apologies," she said sincerely. "I'm very pleased you remembered."

"I wouldn't want anything to happen to Boomer if there was an emergency."

Jessi was surprisingly quiet on the drive out of town, causing Chloe to wonder if she was worried about going up in an airplane. Hesitantly, Chloe asked, "Are you thinking about how much fun we're going to have soaring through the clouds?"

"Actually," Jessi said from her spot in the backseat, "I was wondering if we'll be able to see Heaven if we're that high up. After all, don't angels live in the clouds."

"I'm not sure where angels live, but I'm pretty confident it's a lot higher than the clouds we can reach by airplane. I'd think that Heaven—and the angels—are even higher up than spaceships can go."

"I can't wait to see what it's like inside a cloud," Jessi admitted, her focus pulled from thoughts of angels and Heaven. "Will we be able to see the ground if we're inside a cloud?"

"Probably not, but I suppose it would depend on how thick the cloud is."

"How will Drew see to fly the plane?"

"Why don't you ask him when we get to the farm?" Chloe suggested. "I'm sure he's got a perfectly good explanation."

"Fine. I guess there are some things you don't know after all."

Chloe stifled her chuckle and glanced in her

rearview mirror in time to see Jessi pick up a book and snuggle more deeply into her seat. For now, it seemed, her daughter's curiosity had abated. Thankfully.

For once, it appeared not knowing everything was a good thing.

Drew was waiting on the front porch when they arrived. She'd barely put the car in park when Jessi was unbuckling her seatbelt and reaching for the door handle.

"Welcome, Ladies," Drew greeted. "Come on in and grab a seat. Sam's already at the table and— trust me—he's back to his usual crotchety old self.

"I'm not sure whether that's a good thing, or a bad thing," Chloe commented as they climbed the front stairs.

Drew let loose a long sigh. "It changes from one minute to the next."

Jessi wasted no time making her way down the hallway and into the kitchen, Chloe following closely behind while Drew brought up the rear.

"Good morning, Mr. Morgan," Jessi said, turning full circle in the huge kitchen before coming to a stop at Sam's side. "I'm glad you're feeling better."

"Morning, sprite," Sam returned. "And, if it's

okay with your mother, you can call me Sam."

"Sam would be acceptable," Chloe confirmed. "As long as it's said with respect."

Inhaling deeply, Jessi commented, "Something sure smells good."

"It's that fancy egg dish Andrew's making. Frippy-something-or-other."

"Frittata," Chloe and Drew responded together, their unison response drawing out Drew's laughter.

"Whatever," Sam groused. "Seems like an awful lot of trouble for scrambled eggs." Waving toward the counter, Sam added, "Look what the upstart did. He got rid of my enamel coffee pot and replaced it with that... thing."

"A drip coffee maker?" Chloe clarified. "How nice. At least he didn't get you a cappuccino machine."

"A what?" Sam asked.

"Never mind," Drew put in. "That old enamel pot reached the end of its better days when I was a boy. No doubt it was going to eventually give you lead poisoning. This glass carafe is much safer. And, it's a heck of a lot easier to use."

"The coffee wasn't bad," Sam conceded. "At least not the first cup. We'll see if the second's just as good."

"First though, some juice," Drew suggested. "I

gathered some oranges early this morning and even dug out Aunt Harriet's old juicer to make a pitcher of sunshine."

Sam's chuckle ended in a cough and he pressed his shirt sleeve to mouth to bury the sound. Once the cough subsided, he explained, "She loved her citrus trees, that's for sure. I remember her first real harvest. We had 'sunshine'—what she called her juice—for days."

Once Chloe and Jessi had taken their seats, Drew poured everyone a glass of juice and then returned to the stove.

"Is there anything I can do to help?" Chloe asked.

"Nope, I got it under control. The frittata is coming out now, but it needs to set for a couple of minutes. I'll make the toast while it cools down." He paused for a heartbeat before asking, "No food allergies for either of you, right?"

"No," Chloe confirmed. "At least none that we've experienced."

"Good. I'd hate to have to alter a time-honored recipe."

Within minutes, Drew had placed the casserole on a trivet in the center of the table, and returned to the counter. His back to her, Chloe couldn't see exactly what he was doing. However, there were bowls set along the counter and a jar of honey off to the side.

"Here you go, Jessi," Drew announced as he came toward the table carrying a couple of small plates. "Your toast." Laying a plate in front of Sam as well, he added, "And yours. Just the way you like it."

Jessi's wide-eyed stare turned toward the toast he'd put in front of her. "What kind of toast is this? It's got green stuff on it."

"That's avocado toast," Sam said proudly. "Made from our first pick of the season."

Chloe met Drew's grin. "How very... modern."

"Modern doesn't have anything to do with it," Sam mumbled. "Avocado farmers have been eating our toast like this for decades."

"Go on, Jessi, take a bite," Drew encouraged. "If you don't like it, I'll make you another slice with honey or jam."

"I do like guacamole," Jessi admitted. "I guess I could give it a try." Tentatively, she raised the toast to her mouth and took a small bite. Then another. "Wow! This is great," she declared. "Really, really yummy."

Turning in Chloe's direction, Drew suggested, "If you don't mind, why don't you dish up the eggs while I make some more toast and pour the coffee?"

Chloe got to work, dishing up Sam and Jessi's eggs first, then filling her own plate and Drew's. As spicy and good as the eggs smelled, she was anxious to get her own slice of toast to see if Jessi's assessment was on the mark.

"What's in the avocado mixture?" Chloe asked.

Drew set a platter filled with toast on the table. After refilling Sam's cup and pouring a coffee for himself and for her, he took his seat.

"I'd say, 'it's a family secret', but one taste and you should be able to figure it out. It's very basic. Mash the avocados until they're silky smooth, add a pinch of kosher salt, some finely chopped nuts—in this case, walnuts—and spread on thick-sliced, toasted bread. Then, drizzle with honey. Easy, peasy."

Chloe lifted her first slice in a quick salute before taking a bite. "Oh my gosh. This is delicious."

Sam and Drew smiled broadly, one expression mirroring the other.

"Glad you like it," Drew commented. "The secret is in the quality of the ingredients. Obviously, you need perfect avocados. And, the bread has to be firm and thickly sliced. My preference is sourdough, but a nice multi-grain will do in a pinch."

"May I have another, please?" Jessi asked.

"As soon as you eat some of your frittata," Chloe

explained. "Then, you can have one more piece."

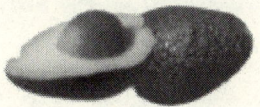

While they waited for Helen to arrive, Drew offered to give them a tour of the barn and surrounding yard. It pleased him when both Chloe and Jessie eagerly accepted.

"If you'd like to, Jessi, you can help me gather some eggs from the hen house."

"You have chickens?" Jessi responded, her voice more of an excited squeal.

"Yep, seven at the moment. All egg layers." Motioning toward the railing of the porch, he instructed, "If you want to grab the basket, we can get to work."

"Oh, fun!" Jessi squeaked. "I can't wait."

"We'll cut through the barn," Drew explained. "The coop is closest to the back door. Then, we can circle around and take a peek at the fruit trees."

Drew led the way, with Jessi practically stepping on his heels in her excitement. Chloe, he noticed, kept pace a few feet behind them.

"Do you have animals, other than the chickens?" Chloe wondered.

"No, not at the moment. We used to have a few horses, two we used for pulling the crop wagon, the other was mine for riding."

"You know how to ride a horse?" Jessi asked.

"Yes, I do. Riding was one of my favorite past times growing up. Until it was time to muck the stalls, at least."

"Yuk," Jessi said, her cute button nose scrunching up and drawing his laugh.

"Yuk is right. Nowadays we use the barn for storing supplies, and parking the two tractors to keep them out of rain and heat. The flatbed wagons are stored at the side."

Chloe stopped long enough to take in the width of the barn before asking, "How many wagon loads will you get from the first harvest?"

"Probably three. Maybe four if the weather cooperates. Then, we'll hand sort the avocados by size. Those that aren't as perfect as we'd like them will stay with us. The rest will go out in shipments to fill our first orders. What's left will go to the co-op."

"There was definitely nothing 'imperfect' about the avocados on our toast this morning," Chloe complimented. "Those were about the creamiest avocados I've ever eaten."

They left the barn through the back door and Jessi made a dash for the fenced-in chicken coop. Drew slowed down until Chloe stood at his side.

"Plenty Good Farms definitely puts out good

quality. Our yield isn't what it once was, but you won't find a better product anywhere."

"Why doesn't Sam replace the crops he lost in the drought?"

"Truthfully, as much as he loves this farm, the last thing he needs at his age is to expand the size of his fields. He doesn't need the money, so why increase his workload when it's not necessary."

"That makes sense, on a personal level. Especially if there's a chance you'll be leaving in less than three months, as planned."

"He keeps reminding me that—one day—I'll inherit Plenty Good. And, while he also insists it's mine to do with as I please, I know he secretly wants me to keep it going."

"But, as you've already said, you've no intention of becoming an avocado farmer," she reminded him.

Before he could respond, Jessi was waving her arms to draw their attention.

"What are their names?" Jessi called out her question from her spot at the wire fencing.

Drew chuckled and reached for Chloe's hand, intending to lead her across the uneven ground. When she closed her fingers around his, a sudden tingle sizzled its way up the length of his arm. He slowed his steps, wanting to prolong the last few feet of their walk.

"To tell the truth, I don't think they have names," Drew admitted once they'd reached Jessi's side. "At least we never named them when I was a kid. I suppose you could choose names for them if you wanted."

Pointing toward a solid white hen, Jessi announced, "That one's going to be Snowflake." One-by-one, she named each of the seven. *Snowflake, Betty, Alice, Henrietta, Satin, Wilma, and Wheezie.*

"Wheezie?" Drew repeated, when the last one had been named.

"Yeah," Jessi confirmed. "She makes a funny noise when she's pecking at the ground. Kind of like she's got a cold."

"She's probably got some sawdust up her beak," he explained. "Or, she's just showing off."

They'd barely made it to the citrus trees when Helen pulled into the drive, her bright red pickup truck crunching gravel beneath its heavy tires.

"The trees are beautiful," Chloe commented, nodding toward the Meyer lemons along the side of the barn. "I see you've got some space for a garden as well."

"We grow the vegetables we use here at home, along with some herbs that Sam dries for winter. He's got a couple of ghost pepper bushes he's extremely proud of, despite the fact that he can't handle the heat any more without getting wicked bad heartburn."

"Is it time to go flying now?" Jessi asked.

"Yes, it is. If you ladies are ready."

Jessi grasped his free hand in hers and tugged. "I've been ready since really, really early this morning."

"I've no doubt of that, Jessi-girl," Drew admitted. "No doubt whatsoever."

Avocado Toast by Nancy Fraser

Chapter Nine

The small municipal airport just south of Plentiful was a beehive of activity. Crop dusters rolled out from the hangars on both sides of crisscrossed runways.

Chloe tightened the band holding her hair in place at her nape. If she were to admit it, even just to herself, she was as excited as Jessi about today's new adventure.

"So, where is your plane?" Pointing off to the side of the closest hangar, Jessi asked, "Is it one of those?"

Drew drove past the planes in question and then pulled in next to a private hangar. "No, Jessi. *Big Bertha*'s not that fancy. Those planes seat eight or ten."

"You name your plane, but not your chickens?" Jessi's incredulous tone gave them both a hearty chuckle.

Once he'd cut the engine, he stepped out of the car and opened Jessi's door. "I didn't name the plane, either." Drew ushered them inside. Nodding toward a gleaming white plane sitting in the middle of the open space, he announced, "Ladies, this is *Big Bertha*. She's a Cessna 172R Skyhawk, a single-engine, fixed-wing aircraft."

"She's beautiful," Chloe told him honestly. The plane looked brand new, even though she knew it wasn't. Obviously, it had been well cared for over the years.

Jessi circled the plane, looking intently at everything within her line of sight.

"The plane was built in 1998 and my aunt bought her in 1999. Other than one landing at the farm, Bertha's been housed here ever since."

"A landing at the farm?" Chloe asked.

"There's a stretch between the lower fence and where the fields start. Harriet always claimed it was long enough to build her own runway."

"I take it Sam didn't agree."

"I think he was worried she'd want to pave it over and he had no intention of covering his precious dirt roads with asphalt or cement." Drew's low chuckle preceded his next words. "Sam and I were working in the south field late one afternoon when we heard the sound of an approaching plane. At first we thought it was one of the local crop dusters passing overhead. Yet, it kept getting closer and closer. We came out from under the trees and—sure enough—there was Aunt Harriet setting the plane down on the dirt road. Neat as a pin."

Chloe followed along at Drew's side as he made a visual inspection of the outside of the plane, checking the prop, the underside of the wings.

"Yet, he didn't let her use the road for her runway?"

"I think she only did it one time to prove her point. Given it took her a good week to get the dirt out of the wheel covers, I doubt she would have bothered again."

He opened the outer door, and lowered the stairs before asking, "You ready, Jessi."

"You betcha."

Drew gave Jessi a lift up to the first stair. Once she was inside, he offered Chloe his hand. "The first step's a bit of a stretch."

Once they were seated and strapped in, Drew passed out headsets.

"We'll get to listen in?" Jessi asked.

"Yes, but there's no microphone on your headset, Jessi-girl, so you won't be able to talk back to the fellows in the tower."

Chloe settled her headset in place, making note of the fact that she did have a microphone. Not that she'd know what to do with it.

Drew put his headset on and then pressed the ignition button. The propeller stuttered once or twice before beginning full rotations. Within minutes, they were taxing out of the hangar and onto the tarmac.

Chloe motioned for Jessi's silence while Drew communicated with the tower. With every exchange between Drew and the ground controller, Jessi's eyes lit with fascination. Chloe imagined her own excitement was just as evident.

Barely ten minutes later, they were airborne and turning west, away from the sun.

"We'll circle around and start south of town where most of the apple orchards are located, then go northwest until the sun's overhead before starting back east," Drew explained. "I'll fly as low as I can so you can choose the landmarks for your videographer."

Drew pointed out areas of interest, and alerted her when they'd moved from one farm to the next. When he reached for her hand, she gladly accepted, loving the feel of his long fingers enveloping her smaller ones.

His touch felt secure, comforting, and gentle.

"What's that?" she asked, pointing off the right.

"That's the old grist mill," he told her. "It hasn't been in operation as a mill for a couple of decades. It was used at one time as a wedding and reception venue. The owners moved away about ten years ago and it's sat vacant since then."

"It's a beautiful piece of property," she commented absently.

"A little overgrown, but the building itself is probably in good shape."

"It would make a great place to hold marketing events," she conceded. "The attraction of the building itself, along with the right product could pull people in from all over the state."

Settling back into her seat, Chloe let the idea percolate. Making herself a mental note to look into the property's availability, she shifted her attention to the upper edge of Sam's property off to the right of the plane.

Within a half hour, they'd turned east toward town, the sun now safely overhead. Drew pulled back on the stick, and the plane rose slowly.

"Want to see the inside of a cloud, Jessi?" Drew asked.

"Um... yeah... I mean, yes, please."

"Just don't knock any angels off their clouds," Chloe warned.

"I'll do my best," Drew responded with a chuckle.

"Aw, mom," Jessi groaned. Yet, the moment

they flew into a few wisps of cloud cover, Jessi was shifting side-to-side with anticipation. "Mom said I should ask you to explain how you see to fly the plane once we're inside a cloud."

"I have instruments to guide me," he explained, pointing to the myriad of dials on the front panel. "This one tells me that I'm flying level. This one, the direction I'm flying." Pointing to the center dial, he asked, "What do you think this one tells me, Jessi?"

Leaning as far forward as her seatbelt would allow, Jessi responded, "It looks like the gas thingy in mom's car."

"Exactly. It tells me how much fuel we have, so we're never at risk of running out."

Chloe motioned for Jessi to sit back. "Settle in, sweetie. We're on our way back to the airport."

Drew began his descent, pulling them out of the clouds, circling across the last of the lemon orchards. The early yellow fruit shone almost as brightly as the sun overhead. If she closed her eyes, Chloe could almost smell the fragrant blossoms.

"Plentiful Tower, this is Cessna, November-one-zero-seven-two-Golf-Foxtrot requesting permission to land on runway two-niner."

"We hear you, Drew," the man's voice responded. "You're clear to land, runaway two-niner."

As smoothly as the takeoff had been, when Drew set the plane down on the runway, it felt as if they were still floating weightless above the ground. Chloe let out the breath she'd unconsciously drawn.

"Nice job," she whispered.

"Have we landed?" Jessi called from the backseat. "I thought it would be bumpier than that."

"What can I say? I've got a soft touch."

Chloe's heart did a little flip. The thought of being the recipient of Drew's 'soft touch' made her breath catch.

They taxied back to the hangar. Steve Porter, owner of the small cargo company where *Big Bertha* was housed, waited for them.

"How was the flight?" Steve asked as he helped Jessi from the plane.

"It was the best," Jessi gushed, her voice pitched with amazement. Turning to where Chloe and Drew were exiting the plane, Jessi asked, "When can we go flying again?"

"Whenever your mom says it's okay," Drew confirmed. "We could make it a regular Saturday date. At least for the next couple of months."

"We'll have to see. After all, we've both got jobs to consider. And, it's not fair to leave Boomer in his kennel every Saturday, when it's the one time during the week when the two of you can spend the entire day together."

"Oh, yeah," Jessi said with a sigh, her previous excitement deflated slightly. "I don't want to hurt Boomer's feelings."

"I bet Boomer would enjoy the farm," Drew suggested. "He'd be able to run from one end to the other. You could even introduce him to the chickens. By name."

"Thanks, Drew. That sounds like a lot of fun. Doesn't it, mom?"

"Yes, sweetie. It does."

"Why don't you ladies meet me at the car? I need to settle up with Steve for the fuel and maintenance charges."

"We're going to poke around the outside of the hangar, if that's okay. There's a vintage plane sitting out back that Jessi wanted to see."

"Be careful where you're walking," Steve chimed in. "I stretched out some hoses along the side wall. I don't want you tripping over them and getting hurt."

"We'll be careful," Chloe assured him.

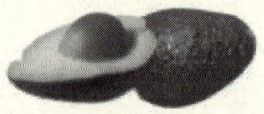

Drew pulled into the driveway next to Chloe's car, reluctant to let this near perfect day end.

"Would you ladies like to come inside for a quick

lunch?" Drew offered.

"I'm starving," Jessi said quickly.

"Thank you," Chloe added. "But I think we should head home. As hungry as you may think you are, Jessi, imagine how hungry Boomer must be."

"I fed him before we left," Jessi noted.

"Yes, but that hound is a canine garbage disposal. He's probably chewing on his kennel, as we speak."

Drew smothered his grin, then suggested, "Jessi, if you want to take a quick peek at the chickens before you go, I'd like a minute to talk to your mother."

"May I?"

Much to his relief, Chloe nodded her permission and Jessi set off for the backyard.

"You wanted something?"

"Oh, I definitely want something." He purposely wagged his eyebrows in a comical leer to emphasize his words.

In return, Chloe shot him a teasing frown. "Is that so?"

"However, I'd settle for a date. A real one. Just you and me."

"That sounds wonderful. I can't remember the last time I went on a date," she admitted.

"How about dinner, Tuesday evening?"

"I'll have to see if I can get a sitter, but Tuesday should be fine."

"You could always bring Jessi and Boomer here for the evening. She and Sam can keep each other company."

"I'm sure she'd love it. It would have to be an early evening though, because of school the next day."

"Early's good for me, too. At least during the week. Sam has me up and out in the fields before seven." He paused, then added, "Who knows? If this first date works out, maybe we could try a Saturday night. A late date. All grown-up like."

"Hmm. Grown up dates are my favorite kind."

Her coy smile curled his toes.

"Mine too," he confirmed.

"So, a date. That was all you wanted?"

"Well, that and maybe this…"

He lowered his head and pressed his lips gently against hers. When he met no resistance, he leaned closer, putting more pressure on the kiss. Chloe laid her hands flat against his chest and he wondered if she could feel the thump of his heart.

When he raised his head, she whispered, "That was nice. Really nice."

The sound of Jessi's sneakers crunching across the driveway gravel broke them apart, and Drew took a step back.

"Maybe we could have a repeat performance after dinner on Tuesday."

"Perhaps."

Smiling broadly, he whispered, "We could consider it dessert."

Avocado Toast by Nancy Fraser

Chapter Ten

"That's the third outfit you've tried on," Jessi pointed out. "I was dressed an hour ago." Narrowing her gaze, she added, "You're going to make us late."

Chloe cast one last glance toward her closet, satisfied with her final decision. Perhaps. She was about to reach for a different blouse when Boomer came crashing into the room, tumbling across the hardwood floor and rolling on his belly.

"See," Jessi said impatiently, "even Boomer's anxious to get going." Reaching down to pet her playful pup, she explained, "I've told him all about the farm, and the chickens, and even told him about Mr. Mor... um... Sam."

"Okay, I'm ready," Chloe insisted, making a cursory check in the hallway mirror as she passed. "Let's go."

"What's so special about going to dinner with Drew, anyway? He's just a regular guy."

"He's a very nice, regular guy. And, it's fun to get dressed up and go out for a change."

"You're not going to kiss on the first date, are you?"

Chloe bit the inside of her lip, forcing back an outright laugh. "Would that be a bad thing? Besides, you were the one that brought it up the last time you mentioned Drew and I dating."

"Yes, I did, but kissing is yucky."

"Spoken like a true eight-almost-nine-year-old. Wait a few years—until some cute boy catches your eye—and you'll change your mind."

"I don't think so," Jessi said, eyeing Chloe with suspicion. "At least not until I'm old, like you."

"We'll see. In the meantime, how about you get Boomer into his car harness? And, don't forget his leash, too."

"Drew said he was making burgers for me and Sam. Do you think he'll make one for Boomer, too?"

"I'm not sure about a burger, but I've no doubt Boomer will be fed as well," Chloe confirmed.

Once Sam and Jessi were served their burgers, salad and milkshakes, and Boomer had received a bowl of his own, Chloe issued her final instructions to her daughter.

"Don't forget to take Boomer out for a walk before it gets dark. He's to stay on the floor when he's inside, not on the furniture. And, most importantly, you're to listen to what Sam tells you and not be a bother." Giving Jessi her sternest motherly expression, she confirmed, "Got it?"

"Yes, ma'am. I'll clear the table, walk the dog, and be on my best behavior. I promise."

"I know you will, sweetheart. It's part of my job as your mother to issue the reminders."

"Don't worry about the sprite," Sam mumbled around a bite of burger. "We'll get along just fine. I'm going to teach her how to play checkers."

Drew stopped at the end of the table where Sam sat. Leaning over, he whispered something in his uncle's ear.

Sam's gaze lifted and narrowed into a glare. "Mind your own business, Andrew."

Offering Chloe his arm, Drew suggested, "How about we get out of here? The smell of those fried onions is making my stomach growl."

"Mine too." Tucking her arm in his, she responded, "Yes, let's go."

Once Chloe had settled into the passenger seat, Drew closed her door and circled the car. Despite his claim of being hungry, getting some alone time with Chloe was his first priority.

"Ready to go?" he asked when he slid behind the wheel. "The drive to Stirling is roughly twenty minutes."

"Are you sure Sam's okay with watching Jessi?" Chloe asked. "I don't want to impose."

Drew pulled out onto the road before confirming, "It's no imposition. As a matter of fact, I think he's as excited as Jessi about her visit. And, he certainly took to Boomer right away."

"I'm curious. What did you whisper to Sam just before we left?"

A snicker preceded his response. "I warned him not to cheat. He has a tendency to make up his own rules as he goes."

"Sam may be in for a surprise. Jessi already knows how to play checkers. Now, we're working on chess."

"Chess? I'm impressed."

"Don't be. I might know the rules and the moves but I'm no master."

"We'll have to play sometime," he suggested. "I haven't played in a couple of years, but it used to be the game of choice in between assignments or during downtime when we were deployed."

"I'd like that, assuming we can squeeze it in before you go back to Texas. I know Sam plans on keeping you busy while you're here."

"Don't worry, I'll always make time for you. And Jessi."

Chloe laid her hand over his, the warmth of her touch easing its way up and down his arm.

"When do you go back for another check-up?"

"Friday, actually. The results will be back on the x-rays, MRI, and bloodwork, so the doctor wants to review everything in person."

"Would you like some company for the drive? As long as we can be back by three, of course."

"What about work? I'd have thought with all the farms in line, you'd have some planning to do."

The tap of her fingers against the back of his hand, sent a shiver across his skin. "I've got everything pretty much in order, at least until the beginning of next week when the co-op featured sales switch over. However, if you'd prefer to go alone—"

"Are you kidding? I'd love some company. Especially if it's you."

They arrived at their destination, a quaint family-owned Italian restaurant, and Drew moved quickly to open Chloe's door.

"Such chivalry," she teased, when he offered her his hand. "You don't see that very often anymore."

"It was the way Sam and Harriet raised me. Faith, family, and kindness."

He gave a gentle tug, pulling her from the car to her feet, bringing them toe-to-toe. Chloe raised her head, her gaze locking with his. The swift dart of her tongue across her full, perfectly-kissable lips made his heart pound, and his breath catch.

"We should probably go inside," she suggested softly.

"In a minute," he whispered. "I've got a sudden urge for dessert before our meal."

Drew lowered his head and pressed his lips to hers. Wrapping his arm around her waist, he pulled her close and deepened the kiss. The delicate shiver of her body against his was nearly his undoing.

He took a step back, putting a small modicum of space between them. The last thing he wanted was for her to realize how easily she affected him. How quickly his body responded to hers. Obviously, she wasn't innocent. However, she *was* deserving of his respect.

"That was—"

"Our cue to go inside," he commented quickly.

"Yes, exactly."

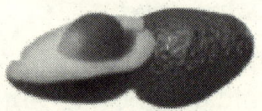

It was just after eight when they arrived back at the farm. Chloe took Drew's offered hand and followed him across the back walkway and into the house through the kitchen door. A light shone above the stove, illuminating a perfectly clean counter top, table and sink.

"So far, so good," she whispered, her gaze scanning the room for anything requiring her attention.

"Sam and Jessi obviously make a great clean-up crew," Drew observed while making the same perusal she had.

When they reached the family room they found Jessi curled up on the couch, her small body wrapped around a huge throw pillow. Her favorite pre-teen comedy played on the cable channel, yet she was struggling to keep her eyes open.

Sam dozed in his favorite easy chair, Boomer stretched out across his lap, a gentle snore coming from them both. So much for keeping Boomer off the furniture.

"Jessi, sweetie," Chloe said softly. "We're back. It's time to go home."

While Jessi gathered up her things, Chloe coaxed Boomer awake and down from Sam's lap. The hapless little pup stumbled over his own paws. A huge yawn ended in a low growl.

"Why don't I get Boomer out to the car and into his harness while you wrestle Jessi into place?" Drew offered.

"Yes, thank you," she agreed. As they walked

toward the door, Chloe complimented her daughter. "You were obviously a big help to Sam this evening. The kitchen was spotless."

"I cleaned the kitchen myself," Jessi explained. "Sam said his arm was hurting, so I did everything except empty the coffee pot."

"His arm?" Drew repeated. "Did he hurt himself?"

"I don't think so. He said it was aching, like from the inside."

Chloe and Drew exchanged glances.

"Well, thank you, Jessi-girl, for taking such good care of my uncle and our kitchen. I'll be sure to empty and clean the coffee pot when I go back inside."

"You might want to let Boomer do his business before we get in the car," Jessi suggested. "I did take him out, but we didn't stay long."

Drew let Boomer off his leash and the pup scurried toward the closest bush.

"Perhaps you should call Doc Taylor tomorrow," Chloe said softly so that only Drew could hear. "Just in case."

"I will. And, I'll make sure Helen can be here on Friday when we drive to San Diego for my follow-up."

"I could stay with Sam if you'd like," she

suggested.

"That's okay. Helen can manage him. Probably better than anyone since my aunt passed away."

With both Jessi and Boomer strapped into their seatbelts, Chloe waited for Drew to reach her side before she opened her door.

"I had a wonderful time tonight. Thank you again for dinner."

His broad grin set a swarm of butterflies loose in her middle.

"Thank *you* for dessert."

Avocado Toast by Nancy Fraser

Chapter Eleven

Chloe wasn't surprised to hear from Drew the next day with an update on Sam's condition. Despite his efforts to get his uncle to see the doctor, Sam had insisted it was only a standard old-age ache and nothing to worry about.

As expected, the stubborn old man had thrown a fit when Drew had insisted Sam stay home and leave the daily orchard work to him.

Despite her own workload, and an appointment with a prospective new group of clients, she'd offered to drive back to the farm and stay with Sam while Drew was in the fields, but he'd assured her Helen was on her way over to help out.

So, now, here she sat in her car—her office away from home—twenty minutes early for her appointment, and giving her presentation one last quick review. With any luck, she'd be able to bring the area's four vineyards into the fold. Their products will be featured at the co-op, along with the produce and honey. And, being able to showcase their properties along with the orchards will make for a stunning video.

"Welcome, Ms Taylor," the young receptionist greeted when she walked through the door of Wishbone Estates Winery. "The group is waiting for you in the conference room."

When Chloe entered the glass-walled meeting room, the first person she spotted was Harley Martin, the VP of Wishbone. The other three men were strangers and ranged in age from mid-thirties, like Harley, to somewhere in their sixties, she guessed.

"Chloe Taylor," Harley said, nodding in her direction. "Let me introduce the fellows. This is Jeremy Priestman from JP Holdings, they own the vineyard next to ours."

The tall man with the striking auburn hair, stuck out his hand. "Nice to meet you Ms Taylor." A distinct brogue tinged his words.

"Please, all of you, call me Chloe," she offered.

"This is Chance Collins, he's the CEO of Collins Winery in Stirling."

Chloe offered her hand to Collins. Tall, good looking, he was close to hers and Harley's age, and likely heir to the Collins Winery fortune.

Nodding toward the last man, Harley added, "And Vince Rossi. He owns Casa Di Vino Winery."

"I'm very pleased to be able to present my ideas to all of you today. I think you'll find I've put together a rather aggressive and comprehensive approach. If it grows in the ground in Princeton County, it should be part of my marketing plan."

Rossi chuckled. "You said she was a smart and confident woman, Harley. You didn't tell us she was a looker too. It doesn't hurt that she's easy on the eyes when you're selling something."

Chloe swallowed back the urge to put the older man in his place for the sexist remark. While she'd never compromise her principles, she knew there was a time and place to correct behaviors, and the start of her presentation wasn't that place.

Once the presentation was over, the four men agreed to meet and discuss the proposal she'd left for them and give her an answer by early the next week. Chloe packed up her briefcase and headed toward the door. Harley Martin fell in step at her side.

"You have to pardon Vince and Jeremy," he said. "They're old school. Chance and I will straighten out their old-fashioned ideas."

Chloe pursed her lips to hold in a laugh. "I'm just grateful neither of them called me 'girlie' or 'missy'. I had enough of that working with the grocery owners upstate."

"I'm glad they behaved. For the most part." He waited for her to set her purse and briefcase in the car before he continued, "Speaking of behaving—or not—we never got around to that dinner I promised you."

"No, we didn't," she agreed. "However, at the moment, the only 'dinners' I'm doing are for my daughter and I, and with a new friend."

"New friend? It would appear, I've lost my window of opportunity."

"We'll see. At the moment, he's only supposed to be here for a few months."

Harley's broad shoulders lifted and fell on a resigned sigh. "Business deal, or no deal, I'll be sure to check back later and see if your situation has changed."

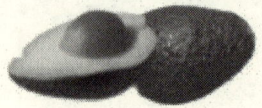

Drew awoke earlier than usual on Friday morning. He needed to get his daily inspection of the crops done before the workers began so he could assign them to the appropriate area for harvesting.

Then, he needed to shower and change clothes before Chloe arrived for their drive to San Diego. Helen was due at nine, Chloe at nine-thirty. With any luck, they'd be on the road by ten, and back home by two, give or take a few minutes.

It was half-past eight when he got back to the house. Sam was waiting in the kitchen, in his usual spot, holding his first cup of coffee.

"What field did you send them to for the morning harvest?" Sam groused. His mood appeared to be as dark as the hot liquid in his mug.

Drew poured a mug for himself and took a seat at the table. "The one you suggested after our drive around last night. Four-north. The Pinkertons."

"Good. I don't want them new fellows making any mistakes and picking before the crop is ready."

Releasing a long sigh, Drew reminded his uncle, "I know what I'm doing, Sam. You taught me well."

"That's why you need to come back for good if those military honchos won't let you go back to active duty. I don't trust anyone but you to run Plenty Good."

"I'm flattered by your trust, even though you seem to be questioning my every decision." He reached for Sam's hand and gave it a squeeze. "I know you're itching to get out in the field. Given you refused to go to see the doc, the least you can do is take his advice and sit back and relax for a week or two."

"How can I relax when I don't know what's going on in my own orchard?"

"Trust, Sam. And Faith. You've put one in me, and one in God. Go with it."

Sam's short nod relieved Drew's anxiety. Somewhat.

"I'll do my best, Andrew. Just know I'll be back in the fields as soon as I'm feeling up to snuff."

"I've no doubt. Now, I've got to get a shower. Helen should be here in time to make you some breakfast."

"I heard you talking to Chloe on the phone last night. Not that I was eavesdropping. Is she going with you today to San Diego?"

"Yes, she is." When the corner of Sam's mouth lifted in a half-grin, Drew asked, "You got a problem with that?"

"Nope, none whatsoever. As a matter of fact, I suppose Chloe and that cute little girl of hers will have an easier job of convincing you to stay than I do."

"We'll see."

"I know you think the military is what you're best at, Andrew," Sam said, his tone low, serious. "But it doesn't have to be. Whether you like it or not, you were a farmer long before you were a soldier."

Drew let his uncle's words sink in. Perhaps Sam was right. Maybe it was time to hang up his uniform for good and come back to the civilian world. As a farmer, or something else entirely. Sam was also right about Chloe's influence. She'd definitely be the biggest bonus to his return.

"Sam looked good this morning," Chloe commented as they were pulling out of the drive.

Drew glanced across the width of the car and smiled. Her concern for Sam was touching. "Yes, he's coming along. Still as ornery as ever, especially cooped up in the house and yard. He even snapped at Helen this morning."

"Really? How did she handle that?"

"She snapped back," he responded with a chuckle. "She's definitely not one to let him get away with anything."

"It's a shame she's married," Chloe pointed out. "They seem perfect for each other."

"From what Sam told me, she and Felix raised five children together on a tight budget. I'm pretty sure Helen can handle anything. Even Sam."

"I can't imagine five children. I can barely handle one."

"You've done a great job with Jessi. She's a sweetheart," Drew told her. "Speaking of great jobs, have you heard anything from the winery group?"

"Not yet. They said early next week, but I was hoping they'd move faster than that. The videographer is anxious to get started and I really wanted to include the vineyards if possible."

"I could give Chance Collins a call if you'd like. Light a match under him, so to speak."

"You know Chance?"

"We went to university at the same time and shared a few agricultural classes. Plus, his wife, Justine, and I dated in high school. A fact he never lets me forget."

Her soft laugh warmed his senses.

"Thank you for the offer. I appreciate it. But, if I'm going to do this, I need to earn it on my own."

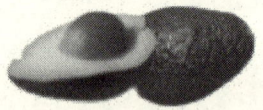

Chloe sat in the waiting room of the military physician's office. She'd read and re-read the one non-military magazine at least a half-dozen times. No doubt she could recite the ingredients for most of the recipes from memory.

She'd admonished herself more than once in the last hour for her thoughts. Her wish that Drew wouldn't be sent back to active duty. Her selfishness surprised her. Shamed her. Yet, she couldn't quite dismiss the feeling that she needed Drew in her life. In Jessi's life.

She was about to check her cell for incoming

emails when the door to the exam rooms opened. Lifting her head, she met Drew's somber gaze. Her heart clenched. As much as she—admittedly—wanted Drew to stay, she also hoped he'd get what he wanted. Even if that meant going back to Fort Hood and leaving her, and Plentiful, in his rearview mirror.

Pushing herself to her feet, she fell in step at Drew's side as they left the office and made their way to his car. Although he'd not said a word, as yet, when he reached out and took her hand in his, she welcomed the warm clasp of his fingers, the steady stroke of his thumb against the back of her hand.

"Well?" she asked, the moment they were seated in the car.

"That's a deep subject," he responded, his sour tone a near duplicate of his uncle's morning demeanor.

"Very funny. Very cliché, but funny."

He started the car, pulled it into gear, and drove out onto the road. As anxious as she was for him to answer, she didn't want to push.

"There's not a snowball's chance in the Mojave I'm returning to active duty. I've got a couple of muscle tears that are never going to fully heal, which makes me unfit for duty. I've been offered a couple of alternatives that the medical staff would agree to without reservation."

"Such as?"

"A couple of standard desk options, the opportunity to teach tactics, and retirement."

"Where would the desk jobs or teaching occur?"

"One for sure back at Fort Hood. The others would likely be on the east coast."

The urge to support retirement sat perched on the very tip of her tongue. Yet, she knew she wouldn't be so bold as to speak up. This was Drew's decision. One he had to make entirely on his own.

"You've obviously got some things to think about."

"My C.O. is emailing me more details. I'll read through them tonight, have a frank discussion with Sam, and then make my decision. Maybe I'll talk to the reverend for some additional guidance."

"Reverend Watson is a wise man," Chloe agreed. "No doubt he'll suggest the power of prayer, and remind you of your upbringing with Sam and Harriet."

"I have to admit, I was fairly certain of what was going to happen during this appointment, so it didn't come as a huge surprise. I have been thinking—and praying—about it ever since my first meeting with the doctor a couple weeks ago."

"And have you come to any conclusions?" Her

heart hammered waiting for his response.

"There are definitely some advantages to packing it all in and staying in Plentiful." He reached for her hand and gave a gentle squeeze. "You among them."

"You'll not hear me complaining," she admitted softly. "However, it's still got to be what you want. Otherwise, it'll never work."

Avocado Toast by Nancy Fraser

Chapter Twelve

On Monday morning, Drew poured himself a second cup of coffee and went in search of Sam. It wasn't like his uncle to not be sitting at the breakfast table when Drew returned from the morning tour of the orchard.

Tapping on Sam's door, he called out, "Sam, you awake?"

"Yeah, just getting this shirt on. Danged shoulders are bothering me."

Cautiously, he pushed the door open. Sam sat on the edge of his bed, one arm through the sleeve of his favorite plaid shirt, the other arm hanging at an odd angle in front of him. Panic clutched at Drew's chest and he rushed across the room.

"Can you lift your arm?"

"Of course, I can lift my arm, it just hurts a bit."

"Let me help you," Drew suggested. "Then, we're heading into the clinic."

"I'll be fine," Sam insisted. "I just need to get some coffee in me."

"I'll pour you a glass of juice for the road, but we're going."

Sam shot him a dark glare. "So that's how it's gonna be, is it?"

"Yes. It is. I can't make any permanent decisions about my own life until I know you're well enough to drive me crazy for a couple dozen more years."

"You can count on that, Andrew. I have no intention of going anywhere but back to work in my avocado fields."

By the time they left the clinic it was nearly lunch. "Chloe's meeting us at the café," Drew explained when he'd turned in the opposite direction of the farm.

"I could use some of Steph's chili," Sam responded, nodding his agreement. "Plus, it'll be nice to talk business with Chloe. At least she keeps me updated on what's going on in town."

"I'd keep you updated too, if I ever got out of the orchard long enough to come into town."

Sam snorted a half-laugh. "About that. I've been thinking about your suggestion to hire a farm manager, in case you decide on one of those options the military gave you."

Drew pulled to a stop in the restaurant parking lot, a few feet short of Chloe's car. "Before you go making any plans of your own, I've asked Chloe to join us for a reason. She was checking on something for me this morning. My plans—or, more precisely— *our* plans may revolve around what she discovered."

"So, you and Chloe have *plans*, do you?" A snicker followed Sam's words.

Rather than respond to Sam's taunt, Drew led the way across the parking lot. They climbed the stairs and entered the restaurant. Chloe was waiting for them in the corner booth.

"Hey, Sam. Drew."

Drew slid into the booth at her side, leaving the opposite bench for his uncle. Beneath the tabletop, he closed his hand around hers.

"Hi there, Chloe," Sam responded. "How's business at the co-op?"

"Steady. We finished setting up the display for our first feature on the avocado harvest. You'll have to come by after lunch and give us your opinion."

"Assuming Andrew here doesn't plan to make me take a nap, or something, I'd like to stop by and see everyone."

The exaggerated roll of Drew's eyes coaxed a laugh from Chloe, and a scoff from his uncle. "I've no intention of regulating your bedtime, old man," Drew teased. "But you will start taking those pills the doctor prescribed, and get yourself on a light work schedule."

"And, if I don't?"

"Then, it'll be back to Fort Hood for me, and you'll be on your own."

"Hmph. So, all I gotta do to keep you here is to follow your rules?"

Pursing his lips to hold in a variety of curse words, Drew met Sam's defiant gaze. "They aren't my rules, Sam. They're doctor's orders."

"How about I share some information on my morning's visit to the realtor?" Chloe suggested. The even tone of her voice offered a welcome respite from his and Sam's verbal sparring.

"Yes," Drew agreed quickly. "What did you find out?"

"The grist mill is definitely for sale, as you suspected. The owners haven't bothered listing it in the past year or two because they'd had no interest previously. However, the realtor assures me they're motivated to sell."

"Most likely to rid themselves of the taxes," Drew guessed.

"You two talking about Walker's old place?" Sam asked.

"Yes," Drew confirmed. "Chloe seems to think it would make a good venue for marketing functions. I'd like to see it used for social functions, the way it used to be."

The waitress came to drop off glasses of water and take their order. Once she'd left, Drew continued. "I suggested perhaps she and I could go into business together. We can buy the mill and fix it up."

"The wineries are on board to join in on the marketing," Chloe explained. "The videographer has the layout for filming. If we could get the mill fixed up by summer, we could do a wine expo with tastings. I'm fairly confident we could draw from all over the state."

Sam's attention shot from Chloe to Drew. "This means you're staying."

Drew nodded. "Yes, sir, it does. I called my C.O. while you were in with the doc and told him to put in my papers."

When he met his uncle's gaze, he was shocked to see tears brimming Sam's eyes. His own heart ached with the joy he could also see in Sam's smile.

"I will need to go back to base and finalize everything, of course. But, I should be back here—permanently—within the next six weeks or so."

"When do you leave for Texas?" Chloe asked.

"Not for a few days. We've still got plenty of time to take a formal tour of the mill, and make our offer if it looks like it'll suit our needs."

"Business partners, eh?" Sam's sly grin wasn't lost on Drew.

"Yes, business partners," Drew confirmed. "For now."

"What about the farm? Will your new business venture take you away from helping me run Plenty Good?"

"We'll work it out," Drew assured him. "Maybe even expand the operation. We could plant that last forty acres you've been meaning to get to since I was a teenager."

Sam gave a sharp nod. "I suppose we could do that, on one condition."

Drew met his uncle's stoic expression with one of his own.

"Oh, look," Chloe said quickly, as if she sensed the two men were about to butt heads. "Our food's on its way."

Once their food was laid out in front of them, not much was said until they were halfway through the meal.

"Well," Drew mumbled around his last bite of burger, "are you going to spell out your conditions, or not?"

"Only one condition, and it's non-negotiable." Sam paused, then continued. "I pay for any upgrades or expansion. If you two are going to sink your money into that old mill, I'll cover the expenses at the farm."

"That sounds fair," Drew agreed. "As long as we agree that part of that expansion comes with a farm manager."

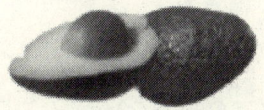

Chloe took Drew's hand while he walked her to the parking lot. His grasp was warm, yet strong and comforting. He stroked her wrist with his thumb, the familiar caress playing havoc with her senses.

She desired this man, more so than any man she'd ever known. Far more than the man who'd given her Jessi. Thankfully, Drew was staying in Plentiful, and taking a bigger role in her life by becoming her partner. First in business, and God willing, on a more personal level once they were ready for the next step in their relationship.

Sam had insisted on paying for lunch and was taking his time shooting the breeze with some of his friends, giving her and Drew a few more minutes alone.

"Sam's over the moon now that you've confirmed you're staying," she commented once they'd come to a stop beside her car.

"It's what he's always wanted. I couldn't very

well disappoint him."

"Well, if it's any consolation, he's not the only one who's happy."

He leaned forward and brushed her cheek with a gentle kiss. "I'm glad to hear that. It makes all these decisions a hundred times easier."

"I know Sam hasn't picked up much extra business after what he lost in the drought. If you need to help him out financially with the farm, I'm sure we can get good financing on the mill property."

Drew pulled in breath and Chloe wondered if she'd overstepped by mentioning family finances.

"Sam's purposely not bothered looking for new business. He's fine with the dozen or so customers who didn't desert him when things got rough."

"Is that enough to sustain a working farm? Especially when he's so generous with what he pays his workers."

"You know about that?" Drew asked.

"Are you kidding? It was one of the first pieces of gossip I heard after moving here. Every high school kid in the area wants to work at Plenty Good for the summer."

"Plenty Good used to be a major producer in the area. However, a few customers who were in it for profit, rather than quality, left for cheaper suppliers.

Then the drought came along and took a few more. What was left was all Sam wanted. Enough to keep him busy and his people employed."

"So, profit isn't important?"

"Not to Sam. Besides, he doesn't need the money."

"Everyone needs money," Chloe countered. "You know... for food... a roof over their head."

"What I meant to say is, Sam's got money. My Aunt Harriet came from money and inherited a small fortune when her father died. Sam, in turn, inherited it all when she passed. He could quit tomorrow and live out the rest of his days in comfort."

"Then, why doesn't he?"

Drew's chuckle was accompanied by an emotional clearing of his throat. "You've seen him out in the fields. He'd be lost without that farm, those beautiful avocado trees."

"If he's happy as is, why expand at all?"

"Because I'll go crazy with nothing much to do, especially after we get our venture up and running. And, someday, it will all be mine and I've either got to go all the way with it, or not at all."

"And, bringing Plenty Good back to its previous glory will make him happy," Chloe guessed.

"Yes, it will. Very happy, in fact. Despite his

insistence that it's enough as is."

"Then, that's all that matters."

"As my aunt used to say, love, family, and faith. The precursors to a happy life."

"A wise woman, indeed."

Chapter Thirteen

Chloe paced around her living room like a caged tiger. Drew was due back sometime today, depending on how early he left Fort Hood yesterday.

The past ten days had been a series of phone calls, lengthy texts, and a couple of video chats. And, with each communication, she'd realized exactly how much she missed Drew. How much she'd come to care for him.

Love him.

Prior to his leaving to settle his military affairs, they'd made an offer on the grist mill property that had been accepted within hours. They'd met with contractors, all of whom had been eager to get to work.

"Mom," Jessi called out. "Are we going out to the farm for supper again tonight?"

"We've been there twice this past week. We're going to wear out our welcome."

"No, we won't. Sam likes it when we visit. He and Boomer really get along. Plus, Sam said Miss

Helen was making another one of her enchilada casseroles."

"Isn't that the second one this week?"

"Yes, because it's mine and Sam's favorite. He also said we didn't need to wait for Drew to show up and you told him we'd be there either way."

"Why is it, you hear everything I say when I'm talking on the phone, but conveniently don't hear me when I tell you to clean up your storybooks and get ready for bed?"

Jessi's shoulders lifted on an exaggerated shrug and her button nose crinkled. "Maybe that's because eating enchilada casserole and feeding the chickens is more fun than going to bed. Besides, Boomer really likes it there. Even when the chickens squawk at him."

Before she could mount a response, her cell rang and Chloe nearly tripped over the rocker in her haste to pick it up.

"Hello," she responded, gasping for a quick breath.

"Running a marathon without me, beautiful?"

"Never. Ever. Especially the marathon part."

"I'm about an hour out, so if you and Jessi-girl want to head out to the house, I won't be far behind."

"Sounds good. I'll get Jessi and Boomer ready to

go. Jessi's been her usual hyper-anxious self."

"Wear comfortable shoes," he suggested. "I'm going to need to stretch my back after this drive and I want to see the new trees Sam had the workers plant this past week."

"We've got a perfect evening for a walk up the hill. I can't wait."

"I've missed you," he said softly. "See you in a bit."

"Yes, in a bit."

They'd barely made their way into the farmhouse when the sound of Drew's four-wheel drive crunching gravel pulled Chloe back outside.

"That was fast," she called to him from the top step of the porch.

"Once I'd heard your voice, and thought about seeing you, I couldn't wait to get here."

"I was expecting you to be pulling a trailer filled to the brim with furniture," she admitted. "Not just a couple of boxes in the back of your car."

"I donated most of my furniture to the base relief fund. It'll be given out—as needed—to new arrivals moving into on-base family housing."

"That was very generous of you."

"Most of it was stuff I picked up on sale. The appliances stayed with the house. The only piece of furniture I kept was the rocker I'd nabbed from the farm when I moved away. It's being shipped."

"Drew!" Jessi shouted from inside the front door. "It's about time you got here. The casserole is almost ready. I'm helping Sam make a summer salad. Whatever that is."

"Well, I guess you won't know what it is, if you're not in the kitchen, will you?" Drew asked.

"Right." Spinning on her heel, Jessi shouted, "I gotta go."

Drew bent and stretched before climbing the four stairs and pulling Chloe into his arms.

"You should probably stretch a bit more," she suggested.

"Naw," he whispered, tightening his embrace. "You're all the medicine I need."

When he closed his mouth over hers, Chloe melted into his kiss, willingly parting her lips for the sweet invasion of his tongue. The intimate kiss set off warning bells, a reminder that they'd agreed to remain celibate until they'd committed to a more permanent relationship.

However, when Drew held her, kissed her, all thoughts of a chaste romance flew out the window on the wings of an escaped parakeet.

Gently, she pressed against his chest, her hands warming with the simple touch. "Enough... for now. Otherwise, we'll be breaking our own agreement."

Made in the USA
Columbia, SC
14 May 2022

60400250R00093